Meet
Cute
Club

Jack Harbon

Copyright © 2020 by Jack Harbon

Cover by Jack Harbon

ISBN: 9798629865032

Edited by A.K Edits / @AdotKEdits

To anyone turning to romance for an escape. We'll get through this, I promise.

And to Barbara. It still doesn't feel like you're really gone. You told me to write something for you, so this one's for you, Grandma. I hope you like it as much as you liked reading all my awful, terrible manuscripts in the past.

Content Warning

I think it's super important to be aware of what you're consuming, and it's never my goal to trade my readers' safety for an unexpected twist or shocking moment. Because of that, I feel it's necessary to include a list of possible triggering content that could potentially upset readers. If you want to go into this story without any warnings, you're more than welcome to skip this page. ♡

Meet Cute Club contains the following:

- Alcohol and/or drug use/abuse
- Mentions of child neglect
- Mentions of homophobia
- On-page sex scenes

One

Claudia's entire body was aflame, the fire deep within her only stoked further by Darren's rugged hands on her hips, travelling higher and higher over the curves of her body. He cupped her face and stroked her smooth ebony skin with his weathered thumbs, careful not to cause any harm. He was still learning his strength, after all.

It required all he had not to let his monstrous instincts take over.

Had this been anyone but Claudia, *his* Claudia, he might not have fought so hard to protect her. In another scenario, his fangs would spring free, and he'd rear his head back before going in for the kill. But this was no ordinary woman. This was the woman he'd spent his childhood with. The woman he'd loved for years. He couldn't possibly imagine

1

hurting her.

Not unless she asked for it. Begged for it. And with how her body practically vibrated with anticipation, Darren could infer that she wasn't far from doing exactly that.

"Please," she whispered, her bare breasts rising and falling as her breathing grew quicker—shallower. Her desperation was palpable, a kind of ache comparable to none. There was no logical explanation for her lust.

She knew the man Darren was. The horrible things he'd done. The trail of bodies he'd left in his wake. None of it mattered. The last thought in her mind was how similar Darren was to a loaded gun with no safety. His imposing presence overtook her senses, and she found herself dizzy, falling for him like she was fifteen all over again.

"Tell me you want me," he murmured against the side of her neck. God, what he wouldn't have given for just a taste. The thudding, throbbing pulse against her throat made his cock harden and his jaw clench with unimaginable desire.

"I need you."

Three words. Three simple, delicious words, her longing fully realized. They sounded even more erotic falling from those plush, pouting lips. Darren slipped one hand around the back of Claudia's head and threaded his fingers through her silken hair. In a low, animalistic rumble, he ordered,

"On your knees for me."

She obeyed, just as she always had. Claudia eased herself onto the carpet, hazel eyes trained upwards in complete submission. Darren ached in his trousers, but not for long. In a matter of moments, he undid the belt and button, unzipping and stepping out of the only thing keeping him moderately decent. Impossibly enough, he didn't feel vulnerable completely naked. Claudia struggled to understand it. He seemed even more confident, more assured in his power.

"Now," he said, gripping the base of his length. "Open your mouth for me, Claudia. I need you to—"

"Next!"

Jordan's head snapped up at lightning speed, reeling as reality came rushing back to him. He stood in the deli line inside McDaniel's Grocery, his nose buried in the latest Patricia Hayes novel he'd picked up last weekend. For just a moment, he'd forgotten where he was, but as he was pulled from the intensity of Claudia and Darren's scene together, it all came back to him.

The slightly fishy smell of the lobster tank a few feet away. The humming buzz of the LED lights overhead. His cart with one cockeyed wheel spinning in whatever direction it wanted rather than the one he needed to go.

Behind the counter, a red-faced Tony stood with his

hands on his hips, judgment etched into the deep wrinkles on his forehead. "I swear to God, Jordan," he muttered.

"What?" It was an innocent enough question, but Tony only glared at him as they'd had this discussion countless times before.

"I called your name about five times. You had your nose buried up that book's ass like you always do. Next time you do it, I'm just gonna start throwing salami slices at you. Maybe then you'll start living in the real world with the rest of us."

Tony meant well, as most people who'd repeated the same obnoxious advice always did, which was why Jordan was able to keep his eyes from rolling or his breath escaping in an irritated puff of air.

There was nothing wrong with him. In fact, he often wondered why it was that more people weren't as obsessed with these stories as he was. Angsty romances involving lifelong friends, vampires that were portrayed as the monsters they were, and countless bloody murders? Every box of his was checked. He just needed more people to get up to speed.

"Why live in the real world when I can be around much more interesting people in these books?" Jordan asked as he approached the counter. He leaned in to examine the various meats and cheeses they'd added to the menu.

"You miss out on life when you have a book in your face," Tony replied.

"Maybe. But I work all day, and then I go home to my fish, Tony. I eat honey-baked ham and cheese sandwiches for dinner every other night. I do my laundry for fun. Let me just have this one exciting thing in my life," Jordan said, grinning.

Tony put his hands up, palms out. "Fine, fine. I'm just saying. You put that book down, and you'll start seeing that there's exciting things out here in the real world, too. You just have to know where to look for them."

Jordan pointed to the meat and cheese that he wanted two pounds of, and Tony got to work, slicing and packaging them for him. Jordan leaned against the counter, slipping his bookmark between the pages of his book and carefully placing it in his cart. Nothing ruffled his feathers more than bent corners and crinkled pages.

"Here you go, buddy," Tony said, handing his order over the counter.

"Thanks. Same time next week?" Jordan asked, the corner of his mouth tugging up into a wry smile.

"Get outta here."

Laughing to himself, Jordan made his way to the register to pay for the groceries he'd picked up. It took everything in his power not to stop by the pharmacy section and peruse the newest books that had been added. He knew from experience that McDaniel's restocked the shelves every Tuesday, and the last time he'd been to the store was the previous Friday. Still, Jordan kept his resolve and pushed forward, swiping his card and thanking the cashier on his way out.

He couldn't blow all his money on more books when he had an ever-growing stack sitting on his nightstand and the book club to worry about.

"Shit, the book club," he said to himself. He nearly ran over a small child with his cart as he hurried outside to his car.

As he climbed into the driver's seat, he scolded himself for being so airheaded. This wasn't like him. In any other given event, Jordan would have been more organized than this. He kept an agenda in his back pocket and religiously scribbled down any date or fact he wanted to remember, no matter how inconsequential or menial. He had nightmares about showing up somewhere unprepared, and when he was younger, his parents had always scolded him for rearranging the kitchen cabinets in alphabetic order.

Jordan Collins didn't *forget* things, and certainly not something as monumental as Meet Cute Club.

Still, he kept his foot steady on the pedal, taking all the shortcuts he could to get to Millerstone, a small bookstore that he frequented more often than most people thought healthy. He blamed Patricia Hayes for his lapse in memory. Her latest release, *Kiss at Sundown*, had consumed the past few days of his life. Unlike anyone normal, Jordan had opted to reread the entire eight-book series again, that way he wouldn't forget a single detail when he finally got his hands on her latest release.

Before climbing out and hurrying inside, he stopped and angled the rear-view mirror at himself. Jordan reached into his center console and removed his car lip balm—and yes, there was a difference between the bathroom lip balm and this one—to quickly coat his full lips. It had been a few weeks since his last trip to the barber, and his hair was slowly curling. Soon, he'd have a head full of kinky black spirals again. Jordan tried not to pay much mind to how dull his typically golden-brown skin looked. The call center he worked at was a life-draining nightmare, but the pay was great.

That's capitalism, baby!

As Jordan stepped through the all-too-familiar doors of Millerstone, he made a beeline for the section he knew like the back of his hand. There, an overwhelming sense of home found him. For so long, he'd felt out of his element, like he was missing something, and this section, with all the shirtless men and couples embracing passionately, rejuvenated him in a way.

Okay, so maybe he was being dramatic.

Was it illegal? No? Exactly.

Jordan put on his blinders and only went after books that he knew he'd need for the club. He found one particular book with the rest of the Christian romances, and he grabbed six copies of those. For the past few months, he'd been covering the expenses for the members of Meet Cute Club. Times were hard for a lot of his friends, and he had disposable income. It was nothing to buy these for them. He liked having their company.

He also grabbed the latest regency romance that they'd agreed to read, followed by a romantic suspense that he'd been most excited for. By the time he was done, he had eighteen books in his hands, and while they weren't all that thick in size, stacked on top of each other, they were two towers in his arms. Carefully, he headed to the register.

This was the part when Carla, the woman who ran the store, would come out from behind the counter and gloat about how right she was when she'd suggested he sign up for a rewards card. He frequented the store so often that Carla joked that he kept them afloat. It was always embarrassing, but unlike Tony, she had a way of making even her critical comments sound sweet.

Instead of the larger-than-life bookstore owner he

expected to see, someone else stepped out from the back room. Someone that made Jordan avert his eyes almost immediately. His dark brown hair jutted out purposefully, like he'd just recently visited a salon, and his beard was survivalist chic, the kind of lazy facial hair that only a few men could pull off and still make sexy. His thin, straight nose was dotted with the faintest of freckles, and his lips were pulled flat into an expressionless line.

The man's intense stare and rugged features made him almost intimidatingly attractive, and Jordan was terrible at hiding his feelings when he became flustered.

"Wow," was all the man said. Jordan glanced at his nametag. Rex. His piercing green eyes bore into Jordan's brown, and he reached for the first stack, pulling it close to him. "You making deliveries to some old ladies?"

Rex was immediately amused by the look of offense that crossed his customer's face. He hadn't been working here long, only about a week and a half, but he had a feeling whoever this man was, he was going to be a regular. Everyone had their own addictions, and judging from what the guy had placed down on the counter, his addiction was starting his own miniature library.

"No," he said, adjusting the buttons on his shirt. "Not just old ladies read these books."

Rex cocked an eyebrow toward the ceiling. "Is that

9

right?"

"Yes. It is."

"I dunno. I just always thought guys like you read good books."

There the offense was. The scowl, the lip quiver as he tried to hide his irritation. If Rex hadn't been intentionally trying to get under his skin, he would've laughed. But he had an act to keep up. Something about the way Jordan held himself made Rex want to tease him, to make him upset and get him riled up. It was an innate response, one that had gotten him into plenty of fights with his younger sister time and time again.

Being a bit of a troll was his thing. The only difference now was that poor Jordan didn't seem to know that he was only screwing with him.

"First, guys like me? What does that mean?"

"C'mon," Rex sighed, looking him up and down. Everything about him screamed Type-A, anal-retentive stick in the mud. The way he constantly adjusted his shirt so that it hung perfectly. How he'd straightened out the stacks of books before sliding them across the counter. Even how he stood, back perfectly straight, head up in attention. He might as well have walked up to the counter with a red dot on his forehead. He was an immediate target.

"Whatever. Second," Jordan continued, "what makes

you think that these books aren't good? Or are you one of the people that judges books by their covers and only reads 'literature'?"

Fuck, his indignation was adorable. The way he practically stomped his foot in frustration, mortally wounded by Rex's jests. How his eyes narrowed as he tossed critiques back. Rex cracked a smile and continued to scan each book. "I don't like predictable books, that's all. You always know how these are going to end."

"No, you actually don't."

"Oh, so they don't all end in marriage and happily-ever-afters? They don't ride off into the sunset together? They don't give readers way too high expectations?" Rex paused to bag the books, making sure to mix and match them. Something told him not putting all the copies of the same title in one bag would bug Jordan.

"No. There are plenty of books that end with the couples not having any kids or even getting married."

"But they all end up together, no?"

Jordan rolled his eyes. "All whodunnit books end with a murderer being revealed. All sci-fi books have some sort of alien or robot or whatever. Why are these books the only ones that people like you throw a fit about? Every genre has its rules and norms."

"People like me?" Oh, Rex definitely wanted to hear

where this was going.

"Yeah, people like you. You think you're better than everyone else because you don't read those 'dumb old lady books,' but little do you know? These are great, and you're missing out. These books are for everyone. But I wouldn't expect you to think so. You're too pretentious to enjoy them."

Both of Rex's eyebrows went up, and he genuinely laughed. Never before had he gotten a rise out of someone with so little effort. Clearly, this was a sore subject for the guy. Had he been teased before this? Were these books his safe place? Rex had no idea. All he could decipher was the amount of passion—and now, anger—that seemed to roil inside of Jordan.

"Are you new here?" Jordan asked suddenly.

"Just started last week."

"Makes sense." He paused to swipe his credit card and put in his PIN. "Just a little bit of advice, *Rex*. You're not going to get very many sales if you make fun of everything that your customers read. You should consider finding a different job if it's so impossible not to give your useless opinions about what people spend their hard-earned money on."

Rex leaned forward and placed his elbows on the counter. The corner of his mouth curled upward before he bit down on his bottom lip. "Mm. Any other tips you'd like to give me? I wouldn't want to be pretentious with any of my other customers."

Jordan narrowed his eyes and snatched his receipt from Rex's hand. For the briefest moment, their fingers dragged across one another. Rex could feel the softness of Jordan's, even from such a hasty gesture. He considered holding onto the receipt, keeping Jordan close for a second longer, but he relented.

"I have nothing else to say to you, other than I hope Carla knows how rude you've been to me."

"If you'd like, you can leave a note for her," Rex smirked. The suggestion received the most dramatic of eye rolls. Jordan grabbed his bags from the counter and began marching to the door. Before he could get too far, Rex called out to him.

"I hope you enjoy reading all your grandma books, handsome," he said.

Jordan stopped dead in his tracks. Rex watched as he bristled and turned around. There seemed to be a slow, warm flush crawling up his cheeks, and though he said nothing, Rex could tell that he was flustered beyond comprehension.

There was something about this uptight man that made Rex want to pester him more than he had anyone else before. Was it the passion behind his words, the way he was willing to defend his reading material with his life? The biting remarks that, deep down, lacked any kind of bite for a guy like Rex? Or was it the way his hot blush made his nose and cheeks a soft shade of crimson brown? How he was left wordless, hurrying out of the store without another look back?

Rex could only chuckle to himself as he took a seat. Clearly, Jordan was a regular here at the store. For whatever reason, Rex found himself eager for the next visit. Eager to go toe-to-toe with this snooty, obnoxiously endearing man once again.

As he climbed into his car, Jordan could only repeat the same phrase over and over again.

"Jackass."

That's what Rex was. What kind of sales rep decided to talk trash about the books their customer was buying? Did he want Jordan's money or not? Worse than the irritation he felt for the new Millerstone employee was the self-criticism about how easily he'd gotten pissed off. Jordan hated letting his emotions show. Nothing good ever came from being overly sensitive, yet he still let Rex get under his skin and bother him to the point of being visibly upset.

However, all of that was better than the most disgusting reaction he'd had in the store. His utter and embarrassingly obvious attraction to Rex.

Jordan sat in his car trying his damnedest to shake the feeling, to rationalize that he wasn't that affected by the man's looks, but his resolve was weak, and he inevitably recalled the way Rex had bitten his lip and looked up at him with those eyes. They weren't just any eyes. They were *those* eyes. The kind that hid secret desires just enough to leave the person on the receiving end wondering if it were all in their head.

He couldn't be attracted to a stupid, judgmental jackass like that, but as Jordan put his car in reverse and hastily drove away, his heart never once calmed down. It echoed in his head, just like the word "handsome" had. Handsome? After all the insults, he'd ended it with something that Jordan hadn't been called in a long time. Not since his mother had passed away. Not by anyone other than his grandmother, who, bless her heart, was always trying to set him up with the younger staff that worked at her assisted living facility.

Handsome.

Handsome, handsome, handsome.

Rex's compliment brought yet another sting of heat to his face. The one caveat was that this time, he didn't have to worry about letting his reaction show. Only he knew what the praise had done to him.

With this flurry of emotions racing down the highway inside of Jordan's mind, he headed home, trying to focus on the following Meet Cute Club meeting and not the fact that if this were the opening scene of a rom-com, in an hour and a half's time, he and Rex would be riding off into the sunset together.

Two

The bag of books that hung from the handlebar of Rex's motorcycle felt impossibly heavy, but it reminded him that soon, he'd be able to dive into worlds unlike his own and escape from the monotony of everyday life. He could disappear in the pages of wizards and dragons, serial killers and amateur sleuths, and government conspiracies and political intrigue.

A job at Millerstone hadn't been his first choice. He'd originally planned on working at the supermarket a few blocks from his grandmother's house, but when they told him they weren't hiring, he'd had to come up with a second plan. The tiny little bookstore two miles away was the next best thing.

Carla gave him a chance, and after he knocked it out of

the park during his interview, she immediately let him know that he started that following Monday. It was part-time, something he could do when he wasn't busy organizing and clearing out the decades of garbage Nana Bailey had accumulated over the years.

Pulling his motorcycle into the driveway of her home, he took off his helmet and carried it up to the front door under his arm. Once inside, Rex dropped the helmet by the door and kicked off his shoes. He'd only been staying at the house for a few days, but he still hadn't gotten accustomed to the smell. It was as if the scent of her perfume haunted the place—with just a hint of mothballs.

If she were here now, Rex knew she'd be ushering him into the kitchen and scolding him for being so skinny. He was a growing boy and needed meat on his bones, never mind the fact that he was a few years shy of thirty and eating plenty.

If she were here now, she'd sit him down and make him flip through old photo albums of when he and Amy were kids. How they'd come over and spend the night watching old Alain Delon movies while she waxed poetic about just how handsome that man could be.

If she were here now, Rex would wrap his arms around her and hug her until she laughed and tapped him to let go.

But she wasn't. She hadn't been here in five months,

though it felt like an eternity and a minute at the same time. Rex, like Amy and his mother, had taken her death hard. No one in Sweet Rose had understood how a woman of nearly eighty years could still be bubbling with such life. Even with her limited mobility and a myriad of medical concerns, Dolores Bailey had managed to keep up with the best of them.

But like all good things in Rex's life, eventually, she had to go. She made the decision herself, he believed. Two days before he got the call from his sister, he got one from Dolores. She told him that she loved him and that she was proud of who he was and who he would become later on down the road. It was out of place, but at the time, he'd thought nothing of it.

Two days later, she was gone.

In Rex's eyes, she'd made the decision that her fight was over, and she was at peace. She could finally leave knowing that she'd done her best and loved her hardest and tried to help as many people as she could. If there was ever a better person, Rex didn't know them.

Which was why, as he walked through the empty halls of her home, Rex struggled to keep the grief from breaking through the surface. He'd been strong for everyone else, just as he always was, but coming back here to clean the house before putting it up on the market was proving much harder than he'd initially believed.

Rex tossed the books on his bed and took a seat beside them, closing his eyes and rubbing the bridge of his nose with his index finger and thumb. Work had been easy on him, but his day was far from over. He still needed to begin sorting through all of Nana Bailey's belongings and packing up only the necessary items. On top of that, he hadn't grabbed anything for dinner on the way home, which meant he was left with canned soup in the kitchen or ordering something off any of the thousands of food apps he had on his phone.

He went for the food apps, only minorly cringing at the delivery fees. It should've been illegal to charge that much for a few burgers and fries.

While he waited for his food to arrive, Rex headed up to the attic to begin cleaning. In his mind, tackling the hardest thing first made more sense. Biting the bullet usually led to an easier life later on down the road, something Rex considered much-needed.

He tugged the chain to the light, and soon, the entire room was illuminated from the single yellow bulb. The shadows only made the attic *slightly* unnerving. Rather than considering what—or who—could be hiding in the corners of the room, Rex grabbed the nearest box and took a seat. He rifled through its contents, picking out important items like manila folders and dusty old books.

At the bottom of the box was a broken picture frame. The glass had shattered long ago, but the picture inside remained unmarred. Rex brought it closer to examine the image.

There was a nagging feeling inside of him as he looked at his mother, his father, and Nana Bailey all together. He traced a finger over the curve of his mother's dark hair and tapped each dotted freckle that peppered his skin as well. They each wore matching smiles, but Rex knew the truth, the story hidden just beyond his father's eyes.

On paper, he was the perfect husband. Loving, providing, and considerate, he made it clear that his wife and son were the only things that mattered to him. Family was the foundation to any man's life, and without it, they were often led down less than savory life paths. Anything less than the idyllic family was unacceptable.

Of course, the truth made his father's beliefs laughable.

Behind the scenes, Alan Bailey lived his life on a whim, landing wherever the wind took him. The vows he'd made came with a section of clauses that excused any of his affairs, and his wedding ring was a fashion statement more than it was a commitment to his wife. That was how Rex ended up with a sister seven years younger than him.

Amy was born into a world of chaos, of petty arguments,

broken promises, and secrets revealed. She shook up Rex's entire world, and for the longest time, he resented her for simply existing. As he grew older, and his father left his mother for Amy's, he grew to understand who the real problem was. It wasn't the child of an affair, but rather the man he'd once so passionately idolized.

Looking at the picture in his hand reminded him that all the stories of love he'd been told as a child were exactly that. The idea that two people could spend forever together was bullshit, lies packaged up by *Hallmark* and Hollywood. In the real world, people were selfish. They were liars, cheats, and users. They were people like his father.

The worst part was that they could never admit it. They plastered on perfect smiles and pretended nothing could shake the foundation of their family. But like the glass on the picture frame in Rex's hands, illusions eventually shattered.

Rex tossed the frame back into the box and returned the rest of the trash inside, burying the image exactly where it belonged. This was too much work. Maybe his assumption about starting from the top had been wrong. The attic was a graveyard of dead promises and haunting memories. He'd worry about it later.

Rex pushed himself up from the wooden floor and dusted himself off, suddenly overcome with the feeling of filth. He needed to wash it all away before it became permanent. In the kitchen downstairs, he spent a few moments scrubbing his hands clean. He dried them on the towel hanging from the oven handle, ears perking up at the sound of the doorbell.

Dinner.

Rex's entire mood changed the second he had his meal spread out on the coffee table in the living room. Between the books he'd retrieved from his bedroom and the greasy feast before him, he couldn't decide what to dive into first. He settled on unwrapping a burger and taking a large bite, wiping the corner of his lips with a napkin before he scanned over the titles.

His eyes fell to the three books teetering on the edge of the coffee table. It had been an impulse, really, a move he hadn't truly thought through before making, but he'd grabbed them all the same. They looked severely out of place compared to his other books, yet they called to him the most.

The same three novels Jordan Collins had picked up two days ago.

Rex convinced himself it was just a joke, something he'd bring up the next time Jordan came into Millerstone, but beneath everything, there was a bit of intrigue. What made these silly little beach reads so interesting? Were they

23

seriously good enough to make a man like Jordan get defensive about them?

Part of him couldn't believe it. In his eyes, all these books were just wish fulfilment stories for lonely women who didn't get out much. Bodice rippers, with scantily clad men and women in dresses that always seemed to fall off the shoulder. Yet there Jordan had been, all stuffy and ready to fight him over Rex's comments about the books.

Clearly, there was something to it, and with Nana Bailey's lack of cable and Wi-Fi, Rex had nothing better to do and nothing to lose.

He reached for the historical one first, settling back into the couch and cracking open the spine.

Saturday. The day that, for the past six months, always sent Jordan's stomach into a frenzy. His nervousness crackled like lightning as he flitted all over the house, making sure everything was perfect. To anyone watching through the windows, he must've looked absolutely out of his mind running all over the place, this direction and that. He needed everything to be perfect.

Jordan placed the tray of cookies in the middle of the coffee table, followed by a pitcher of lemonade, six bottles of water, and a stack of napkins. In the kitchen, he lit his favorite lavender vanilla candles, and while the scent began wafting through the house, Jordan twisted the blinds open and parted every set of curtains on the windows.

By the time he was finished, his little house radiated with light. It made his white furniture practically glow. The smell of freshly baked cookies mixing with his candles gave the entire house a feeling of warmth that he knew the members of Meet Cute Club would love.

Right on time, there was the knock of his first guest. He straightened his short-sleeved white button-up, took a deep breath, and unlocked the door, pasting on a wide smile as he hugged Lana and welcomed her into the house.

"Ooh, it smells delicious in here," she said, taking a seat on the sofa in the living room. She placed her bag down on the floor and looked around. "I'm not the first one, am I?"

"You are, yeah."

"Shoot," she said, slouching. "I wanted to be fashionably late so that everyone could compliment me on how much weight I've lost!"

Jordan cracked a smile and looked her over. "You seem happier."

"I am! Have you heard of the keto diet? Seriously, Jordan, it's life-changing, I swear to God."

As she launched into her pitch for this new lifestyle choice of hers, Jordan could only listen with amusement. It seemed every other week Lana was coming up with new things to try and exploring different social groups. It was a miracle she'd stuck with Meet Cute Club for so long, considering she'd joined on a whim, and as her previous track record showed, commitment didn't seem to be Lana's thing.

The other four members arrived during the twenty minutes leading up to the official start time of the meeting, and Jordan hopped up each time to give them a hug and welcome them. Gloria had just gotten her hair dyed, which she was excited about, and Madeline had recently returned from Hawaii for her grandson's wedding, which she was more excited about. Even Charles, the only other man in the group, came bearing good news about his job promotion.

Jordan needed their positivity.

It had been six months since the conception of Meet Cute Club, and since then, their membership had been cut in half. He couldn't hold it against the other five members who'd dropped out for one reason or another, but it hurt every single time. And with nobody filling their spots, each loss picked at Jordan's hope. If they couldn't get their numbers up, he wasn't sure if Meet Cute Club would even be a thing in six more months.

"Alright," he said, smiling. "We're all here!"

They cheered and gave a small round of applause as

Jordan grabbed the large Millerstone bag and began distributing the books. One of the ways Jordan had been able to retain the people he had was by offering to cover the expenses. He had expendable money, and if it took buying fifteen books a month to keep this passion project alive, he was willing to sacrifice.

"I've been looking forward to this all week," Gloria said, thumbing through *The Duke's Deadly Bride*. Regency romance was always her favorite, and she made no secret about her obsession with history and the scandals of old English society.

"I've heard good things about this author, so I'm stoked," Lana said.

"Not to brag," Jordan said, smiling wide, "but she replied and retweeted one of my tweets about this series."

"Shut up!" Madeline exclaimed.

Charles clicked his teeth and shook his head. "You and your luck, Jordan, I swear."

The knock at the front door cut their conversation short. As Jordan rose from his seat, Lana popped up faster. "I got it!" she said, disappearing around the corner.

"Were you expecting anyone else?" Gloria asked, sipping from her bottle of water.

"No, but I'm sure it's just a delivery for more books. I might have a problem," he chuckled. "Sometimes I wish I had another set of eyes to read with."

"Ain't that the truth?" Gloria pulled her hair back into a ponytail, and Jordan was in awe of each curl that she put up. He'd been trying to grow out his own hair, but after the severe damage he'd gotten from dyeing and straightening, it was taking longer than expected. He longed for his natural curls back, but Black Jesus wasn't granting him mercy.

Lana poked her head around the corner with an odd expression on her face. "Hey, Jordan? There's someone here for you. He says he knows you?"

Jordan scrunched up his nose but stood nonetheless, following Lana into the foyer. Immediately, he felt himself tense up at the sight of Rex standing there, hands buried in his ripped-up light wash jeans. In his white tank top, Jordan could now see the sleeve of tattoos trailing down his right arm. His thick hair was brushed back from his eyes, making every feature of his face even more noticeable.

Jordan swallowed hard. *Shit.*

"I'll let you two talk," Lana said. She slipped around Jordan and hurried off back to the living room with the others.

Jordan's initial shock quickly melted into irritation, and he grabbed Rex by his tatted arm, desperately trying to ignore the tight, defined muscles he felt beneath his soft skin as he dragged him into the kitchen. With a low voice, he demanded,

"What the hell are you doing here? How did you even find out where I lived?"

"Carla," Rex said. "Asked if she knew who the nerd was that came in and ordered eighteen romance books. She gave me the neighborhood you lived in, and I figured the house with all the cars in front of it was yours."

"Okay, first of all, Edward Cullen, that's really stalkery and weird. Second, you didn't answer my first question. Why are you in my house right now?"

Rex reached around to his back pocket, and Jordan was treated to another glimpse of his delicious body as his tank top inched up ever so slightly. The glimpse of that v-line was what made Jordan flush and look away.

In Rex's hand was a copy of *The Duke's Deadly Bride*.

"Why do you have that?" he asked.

"Because I'm reading it."

"You're so funny," Jordan said, rolling his eyes. "You said they were for old, lonely women. Why would you be reading it?"

"Because you're reading it. You find it interesting, and I find you interesting, so I wanted to see what it was about." The way he said it, so nonchalantly, as if it were the time or the weather, unnerved Jordan just a bit.

I find you interesting. Jordan shifted slightly, ignoring that remark.

Just a few days ago, Rex had ripped into the entire genre, insulting Jordan and anyone else that had even a mild interest in love stories. Now here he was, showing off his copy? It didn't make sense to him.

"Okay, so why are you telling me all this? Do you want a pat on the back for not being as pretentious as I said you were?"

Rex chuckled, and even with how irritated he was at the man's presence, Jordan found himself quickly falling for that deep, sultry laugh.

"Jesus, Jordan, you act like I personally wounded you."

"Sorry," he said quietly. "I guess I just don't like it when people insult me to my face and then try to be buddy-buddy with me a few days later."

Rex sighed and folded his arms over his chest.

Seriously, he needed to stop doing that.

"Look, I'm sorry for making fun of your little books, okay? I bought this book because I wanted to see what it was all about, and I actually don't hate it."

"Seriously?" Jordan's eyes narrowed.

"Seriously. I mean, the pacing is slow as hell, but it's not the worst thing I've ever read. It's no *Pride and Prejudice*, but…"

"I thought you didn't read little books like that."

"I graduated high school, Jordan. Everyone reads that book in high school."

Fair enough. It was now Jordan's turn to fold his hands over his chest. "So, what now? Are you saying you want to join my silly little book club? Or did you really just come over to ease your guilt about being a douchebag at Millerstone?"

For the first time, Rex's arrogance gave way to something else. His cocky smirk softened, and that playful gleam in his eye disappeared. "Both? I mean, I'm not gonna say sorry about Millerstone because that was funny, but *maybe* I shouldn't have gone so hard on you."

"Yeah, maybe," Jordan muttered. "I just don't really see you joining Meet Cute Club."

"Wow, I thought romance was for everyone."

Jordan wanted to be mad that he was throwing that statement back in his face, but he had a point. If he kept Rex from joining Meet Cute Club, he'd be no better than Rex when he took it upon himself to judge all the books that he read. He couldn't preach about how inclusive the genre was and then exclude Rex from the experience.

"Fine," he said, glaring at Rex. "You can join. But this isn't a joke. This isn't a chance for you to throw all your Devil's Advocate hot takes at us. We're serious about these books here, and you should be too."

Rex's perfect teeth glimmered as he smiled. "Deal."

"I'm serious, Rex."

"Okay! This isn't a book club about kissing. This is serious, serious business."

Jordan groaned and turned around, walking to the living room. Rex followed close behind. When all eyes fell on the two of them, Jordan cleared his throat and said, "Everyone, I'd like you to meet our newest member of Meet Cute Club!"

Rex gave a nod of acknowledgement to everyone sitting around the table. "Hey. I'm Rhett Bailey, but everyone just calls me Rex."

Three

Amy sat back on her haunches and made a show of dusting off her hands. Rex stood at the opposite side of the room, eyeing her down suspiciously. "You done?" he asked.

"I don't know how you do this," she said, looking around at everything in the spare bedroom. Dozens of boxes towered over them, stacked five and sometimes six tall. Rex had to admit that it was excessive, even for Nana Bailey.

"It's a challenge, but it's kind of nice to go down memory lane. Sometimes I forget about all the good things that happened."

Amy had been over twice since Rex agreed to clean out the house, and since her visit the first night he dropped off his bags, he'd spent every night unloading all of their grandmother's belongings and looking through everything she'd accumulated over her seventy-three years. One thing that had surprised him was just how much she loved to collect.

Buttons, pins, bookmarks, and even postcards. Each of her interests got their own special book, where she'd write a little story about how she found the item and why she wanted to add it to her collection. Two nights ago, Rex had holed up with his dinner and spent the entire night reading all about her adventures in coin-hunting.

"Good things happened, Rex. You know they did," Amy said with a sigh. "Your whole life isn't a Charles Dickens novel."

"Fuck off," he laughed, rolling his eyes at her. "That's not what I'm saying. It's just that I've forgotten a lot of the good things that happened when Dad was still around in my life."

"Yeah, well, when it comes to Dad, it's hard to suss out the good memories from the bad ones."

There was a bitterness in her tone that Rex felt deeper than anyone else possibly could. The utter disappointment that their father was. The wasted potential and the crushed dreams. Most kids eventually realized their parents were human. Rex realized that his father wasn't even fit enough to call himself a man.

"How's your mom doing?" he asked, folding his arms over his chest and leaning against one of the sturdier box towers.

Amy picked at her cuticles, almost making it a point to avoid looking at him. "She's alright."

"Amy."

"Rex."

"You can talk to me. You know that."

"I do," she said. After a moment, Amy groaned and let her head fall back. "I hate him, Rex. He's such an asshole! Mom's been making herself sick, that's how upset she is. I hear her every night after dinner, retching in the bathroom. She can't even eat anymore. Not since she found out."

Hindsight was the worst gift Rex had ever received, and listening to Amy talk about her mother's reaction to their father's affair was like seeing his own life play out in front of him. He recalled all the nights spent holding his mother in his arms to keep her from falling apart entirely. The way she'd stared dead ahead of her, eyes glazed over, unresponsive. Alan Bailey must've been a witch or something, because the way he left women spent after he was done with them was something supernatural.

It was cruel, nihilistic evil.

And now, all Rex wanted to do was comfort his baby sister and help her work through this pain. With Georgia being the woman his father left his mother for, it was hard for Rex to muster up much empathy for her, but caught in the middle of all of this was Amy. The person who hadn't asked for any part of this scenario. She was innocent, the one good thing to come from this bad situation, and Rex wanted to strangle his dad for playing a part in Amy's anguish.

"C'mere," Rex said, jerking his head. Almost reluctantly, Amy got up from the floor and dragged herself towards him. Rex pulled her into his arms and rested his chin on the top of her head. She'd just turned twenty-one, but to him, she was still the kid he'd been forced to babysit all those years ago.

"He's just…he's so…"

"I know. He's exactly that."

"Mom is going to kill me if she finds out I told you. So, if you talk to her, don't mention this, please."

Rex couldn't see a conversation between them happening anytime soon, but he still agreed to make her feel better. If there was one thing that he and Amy had inherited from Alan, it was the inexplicable knowledge of what *not* to say. The reaction *not* to give. Playing clueless and keeping tight lips was the way of the Baileys.

"One day, we're going to have to tell them to clean up their own messes," Rex said once Amy stepped back from the hug.

She smiled sadly. "You say that, but look where you are. Standing in Nana's house, cleaning up. Doing what Dad refuses to do. And I spend every night cleaning up my mom's vomit. You're nuts if you think we'll ever stop doing this."

Rex knew the truth should have hurt him. The idea of always being behind his family, picking up the pieces, should have made him sick. The only thing he felt was numb. This was how they'd been raised. This was their world, the way of the Baileys. Some cycles just couldn't be broken. Still, Rex gave his empty promises and preached his hollow words on the off chance that they could offer Amy some kind of solace.

"Maybe," Rex shrugged. "Or, maybe we'll get lucky and get to live our own messy lives."

"The only thing messy that I want is a double bacon cheeseburger from Barney's. Can we go get something to eat?"

"I was thinking the same thing."

"Perfect." Amy looked around at the boxes and shook her head. "I don't know how you're gonna pull all this off."

"Me, either. This is a problem for future me," Rex replied. "Now, you go get washed up."

Amy nodded and headed off to the bathroom. When she

returned, she had his copy of *Duke's* in her hands. She turned it over and read the back, scoffing. "Was this Nana's?"

"Yep," Rex said, reaching for it. Amy turned away and flipped through some pages, stopping at the bookmark. It was a Millerstone receipt with the rest of Rex's order.

"I guess Nana was able to buy books from the grave then, hm?" When she looked at Rex, her tiny, doll-like face was scrunched up suspiciously. "Why'd you buy this? Doesn't really seem like your speed."

"No reason."

Amy cleared her throat and began reading from the intimate scene that Rex had stopped on. When he complained, she laughed and said, "Tell me the truth, and I'll stop."

"Alright, fine. There's this guy."

"Ooh." Amy's brows waggled up and down suggestively. "What's his name?"

"Jordan."

"And you bought this book to impress him?"

"Uh...kind of? He gets in a mood whenever I tease him, kind of like how you do. I thought I'd join his silly little club and make fun of him some more. That's why I have that book."

"You like him, don't you?"

There was no point in lying to Amy. Not when she knew as well as he did what the truth was. "I guess. He's cool, or whatever. Very high-strung. Always tense."

"He sounds terrible."

"You sound jealous."

"Of your boyfriend? Not at all."

"Of me teasing someone other than you," he said, suddenly snatching the book back. "Gimme that."

"Whatever, jerk-ass. I'm ready to go eat. Whenever you're done reading your kissing book, I'll be waiting in my car. Bye!"

"It's not—"

Amy held up her hand and marched out of the room, leaving Rex standing with his book in his hand. He called out to her again, "It's not a kissing book! It's also got some political commentary about the treatment of women and... Never mind."

No use. She wouldn't understand unless she read for herself, and more important than that, Rex wasn't going to defend this book. That was Jordan's role in all this, not his. No, sir. Rex tossed the book onto the dresser a few feet in front of him and hurried out to the car.

Barney's Burger Barn was *the* place to get a classic hamburger and shake combo. Rex had been going to Barney's for as long as he could remember. Standing behind the counter, the larger-than-life man himself grinned wide and waved at him and Amy. His deep brown skin glowed from the red neon light of the sign above him.

"Usual?" Barney asked, looking between them.

"You know it." Rex led Amy to a booth near the front of the restaurant and collapsed into his seat, sighing and stretching. With its vintage aesthetic and jukebox playing Buddy Holly, Barney's was the closest a place could get to the '50s without a pack of greasers threatening Black people and McCarthyism running amok.

Some of the only few fond memories Rex had of his father were attached to this place.

As he and Amy ate, they talked about her plans for finishing up her senior year of college and where she was going to move after graduation. She'd been considering leaving Oklahoma for years, and Rex encouraged her to go. There was so much to explore and experience outside of their tiny little town. The best thing for her would be to get away from home, at least for a few months.

When Rex rose from his seat to get refills for his and Amy's drinks, he did a double-take. Sitting in the back of the restaurant was none other than Jordan Collins, face buried in a book, hand blindly searching for a French fry on his tray.

A tiny jolt ran through Rex, and he turned and hurried

to the counter. Was he…nervous? That didn't make any sense. Not when it came to Jordan, one of the most uptight men he'd ever met. In all of his dating experience, he'd been the calm, collected one. He'd been the cucumber, as an ex-boyfriend would say.

But something about Jordan was different. Maybe it was the way he held himself—confident but not arrogant. Yes, he was a man reading—as Amy had so eloquently put it—kissing books, and fuck you if you had a problem with that. There was something perfectly unnerving about that sense of self-assuredness that Rex could only find himself more and more drawn to. In the grand scheme of things, it wasn't a big deal, but in a place like Sweet Rose, people put weight on the littlest things.

Barney slid the cups back to Rex, snapping him out of his head.

Carrying them back to the table, Amy leaned forward and said, "That's him, huh?"

"That's who?"

"The guy you were talking about earlier."

"His name is Jordan."

Amy tapped her chin and leaned out of the booth to get a better look at him. "Jordan and Rex, sittin' in a tree—"

"You stop that," he warned, pointing at her.

Raising her voice, she said, "What, stop talking about

41

Jordan?"

"Amy!" Rex hissed. "I'm serious. Knock it off."

She fell back into her seat, giggling. This was the exact reason that Rex always made fun of her whenever he could. She messed with him just as much as he did her. "Wait until your graduation day, you brat. I'm going to make it miserable for you."

"Yeah, yeah," she said, rolling her eyes. "Why don't you go talk to him? He's right there."

"He's busy."

"And? I mean, do I have to remind you about the time you almost got us arrested for street racing, all because you wanted to get that one guy's phone number? You've done far worse than bother someone while they're reading."

"Just eat your food," he grumbled, sitting back and picking at his lettuce.

Rex's frustration lay more in himself than anything Amy could've brought up. It wasn't like him to get this way about men around him. In every other situation, he relished knocking them off their game, taking control of the situation and laying it on thick. He left them flustered and blushing, not the other way around. Yet here Rex was, trying not to get caught staring at Jordan from across the room. It didn't make any sense.

"Go talk to him," Amy said after she finished her burger.

"I need to use the restroom. When I come out, you better be over there talking to him." She rose from the table and left without giving Rex a chance to argue. Annoyed, he turned back to look at Jordan. The other man flipped the page of his book and smiled to himself.

It had to be one of the nicest smiles Rex had ever seen.

Mustering up all the arrogance he could, he took a breath before crossing the room.

Even with his eyes glued to the page, Jordan could feel the presence of someone approaching him, and he glanced up to see who it was. His stomach clenched when he immediately recognized him. He knew that tattoo sleeve and self-important walk anywhere.

Rex.

Lovely.

Maybe it was childish, but he still hadn't entirely forgiven Rex for the incident at Millerstone. It wasn't like Jordan to hold a grudge, but these books were his safe space. In a world of bigotry, violence, and injustice, he'd found a place to escape real life, where every struggle and trial the characters experienced led to an ending that made it worth the strife.

Sure, the industry could do with much more diversity and meaningful conversations about representation, but that was a different topic for a different time.

Right now, it was time for *this* guy.

"Hey," Rex said, sliding into the booth across from Jordan.

"Hi."

"Wow, is it cold in here or is it just you?" he teased.

"I'm perfectly room temperature, thanks," Jordan said, putting his bookmark between the pages and tossing the novel on the table. He leaned forward and swirled a French fry around in his pool of ketchup. "Can I help you with something?"

"I just wanted to talk, that's all."

"About?"

"I've been reading *The Duke's Deadly Bride*."

"And?"

"And it's not really my cup of tea," Rex said, shrugging. "I mean, it's fine, but everything is moving really slow. And Hawthorne is an asshole. He doesn't understand boundaries, and he keeps bugging Elizabeth."

Jordan gave Rex a pointed look.

"Hey," he started, cracking a smile. "I'm not an asshole!"

"Okay." Jordan struggled to keep from smiling as well.

"I'm not!"

"If you say so." He took a long sip from his soda before he said, "Are you going to DNF the book, then?"

Rex shrugged. "Maybe? I'm already about halfway

through the book, so I might as well finish, but this isn't exactly what I expected. You hyped it up so much, and I'm just a tad bit let down."

Indignation rattled around inside of Jordan. "I didn't hype this book up. I told you the genre was great, not that every book you'd read was."

"Okay, well, if you know everything about the genre, what should I read after this? I have all the time in the world after work."

This was the moment that always made Jordan's heart flutter. The chance to give someone a recommendation. The hope that filled him when he thought about the possibility of someone else loving the same book as much as he did. But with that excitement came a brief moment of pressure. What if he picked something and they hated it? What if they thought differently of him if he recommended some *weird* shit?

"Patricia Hayes," was all Jordan said.

"Patricia who?"

"Hayes. She writes fast-paced, sexy paranormal romance. I'm assuming you also didn't like how chaste and sweet everything was in *Duke's*?"

A smirk crossed Rex's lips, and he leaned back in his seat. "It was fine. I would've liked something more explicit."

"Then start with Patricia's *Beasts of Brooklyn* series. It

45

covers all the bases. Fast, sexy, lots of blood and action, and there's even an asshole that gets exactly what he deserves. No offense, of course."

Rex licked his bottom lip, and without another word, he pulled his phone from his pocket and slid it across the table. Jordan barely caught it before it fell from the edge and clattered to the ground. His eyes went wide.

"What is this for?"

"Write a few more recommendations down. I'll forget, otherwise."

Jordan took a moment to think before he began listing series names and authors that he thought Rex might enjoy. He steered clear of anything too low-stakes, opting for the dramatic side of the spectrum. Books with intrigue, murder, and scandals. Those happened to be his favorite as well, so by the time he finished, the list on Rex's phone was longer than he'd intended.

"Done?" Rex asked.

"Yep, here you go." He started to hand the phone back when Rex shook his head.

"Put your name and number down in there, too."

"W-what?" Jordan blinked. He couldn't be serious. "Why?"

"In case I have any pressing issues with these books, or the club. Everyone else in the club has your number, right?"

The Cheshire grin he wore told Jordan that this was about more than just books. Was this his roundabout way of flirting or making the first move?

"Okay," he said, quickly creating a new contact and adding his information. He saved and slid the phone back to Rex, slipping his hands underneath the table to wipe the sweat from his palms. He didn't need Rex seeing just how much he affected him. Taking back control of the situation, he produced his own phone from his pocket and handed that over as well.

"Put yours down, too."

Rex cocked up an eyebrow but said nothing. He took a moment to put in his number and handed it off. Jordan reached for the phone, but Rex kept his grip. His eyes grew more intense, and in a low hum, he said,

"Feel free to text me about anything you'd like. Anything."

Jordan swallowed hard and pulled his phone free, placing it on the table. "I'll keep that in mind."

"Please do." Rex reached for a fry off of Jordan's plate, dipping it in ketchup before he popped it into his mouth. "Anyway, I've got to get out of here. See you around."

"Yeah," Jordan murmured, glancing at the woman standing off to the side of the restaurant. She looked remarkably like Rex with her deep green eyes and wild brown hair.

Rex stood up and straightened his jacket, winking at Jordan before he and the woman headed out. Left alone, he relaxed and took a slow breath, trying to make sense of what had just happened. They'd traded numbers under the guise of Meet Cute Club business, but he wasn't naive. He and Rex both knew what the real message was.

Anything.

It had been far too long since Jordan had ever felt his heart quicken this much. At the call center, many women had tried their best to flirt, but when he eventually told them the truth—that they were beautiful, but barking up the wrong tree—the flattery stopped. If he were being honest, he couldn't remember the last time a man had made his interest this apparent.

Sure, Jordan didn't get out of the house much, but he'd tried his hand at various dating apps. None of the matches had lasted longer than a few weeks and a number of traded pictures. Besides, what did he need to talk to other men for? If they didn't make him feel as giddy as the latest Maureen Phisher romance did, what was the point?

Still, Jordan would be lying if he said Rex's forwardness was a complete turnoff.

Rex's intentions were clear, and Jordan wasn't sure how to proceed. Rather than figuring it out, he reached for his phone on the table and scrolled through his contacts. He didn't find Rex's name anywhere in the R section. Confused, he went through every name again. It wasn't until he got to the Ys that he saw a new contact.

"'Your New Favorite'," he read aloud. Jordan couldn't help but laugh. Rex Bailey. The cockiest bastard Jordan had met in all twenty-six of his years living in Sweet Rose. He put his phone away and tried to read his book again, but every thought returned to Rex.

He hated himself for falling for Rex's charms, but damn if they didn't feel good.

Four

"Sherleen Jackson," Jordan said to the woman working the front desk of Garden Views Assisted Living. Jordan had almost been surprised when he stepped up and was asked his name. Any other time he visited his grandmother, the receptionist told him to just head inside. The brunette behind the desk must have been new.

"Ah, there she is," she said, typing on her computer quickly. "She's in room 308."

"Perfect, thank you."

Of course, he was well aware which room his grandmother was staying in, but it wasn't worth pointing out. If this new woman lasted long, she'd eventually get accustomed to seeing him around anyway. Jordan maneuvered through the winding halls of the building, slipping around staff members and residents as they hurried back and forth.

When he reached 308, he knocked rhythmically, letting the woman inside know exactly who he was. A moment later, the door swung open, and he was greeted with the glowing face of his favorite grandmother in the world.

"There my baby is," she said, pulling him into a hug with surprising strength. "I was starting to wonder if you were gonna come today." She situated him on the sofa and had a glass of sweet tea in his hands before he could even blink.

"Sorry about being so late, Grams. I was on the phone with my boss all morning."

"What'd he want?"

"Same old. Telling me I need to do better and work harder," Jordan muttered. "He wants me to take on more responsibilities at work but isn't willing to pay me more."

This had been a point of contention between him and his job for the past few weeks. Every time he started getting used to the additional tasks he was taking on, Jordan's managers threw something else at him. He was working accounts that they were supposed to be dealing with on top of the ever-growing queue of customers needing his help with tech support. Whenever he'd bring up the topic of a raise, they'd change the subject, and he was getting quite sick of being jerked around.

Sherleen sucked her teeth and shook her head. "That's just like some corporate bitches to try and play you like that. Don't let these white men punk you, Jordan, you hear me? Put your foot down and tell them no."

He smiled bashfully. Grams' vulgarity was one of his favorite defining traits about her. "Yes, ma'am."

She reached over and gave his hand a light squeeze. As she opened her mouth to say something else, the oven timer dinged. Reaching for her cane, Sherleen crossed the room and slipped on an oven mitt.

"What's that?" Jordan asked.

"Well," she said, bending over to pull out a tray of muffins. "You remember that handsome man I told you about a few weeks ago? The one that volunteers every now and then?"

Jordan thought back to their conversation earlier. "The one that looks like he could be Terry Crews' son?"

"That's him. Powell Robertson. He's been coming by and giving me new recipes to try out, and I'm starting to feel like Black Betty Crocker out here."

Ever since he'd first started volunteering, Sherleen brought up Powell whenever she could. She waxed poetic about his rich brown skin and his perfect cheekbones and full lips. There were times Jordan wondered if this was just a bit of banter between them, or if she was considering going full-on cougar. There was also the possibility that she was trying to set him and Powell up. He wasn't sure which option was worse.

Sherleen held up one of the muffins. "Try this."

Jordan stepped into the kitchen and took the warm muffin Sherleen handed him. When he bit down, he was immediately hit with the cranberry flavor, and his eyes went wide. Before he knew it, he'd already eaten half of it. "Jesus," he said.

Sherleen gave him a stern look, and he quickly apologized for taking His name in vain. "That's not even the best recipe he's given me, either. I think he's trying to fatten me up so none of these other men want me except for him." She waggled her brow suggestively.

"Oh, so Powell's your boyfriend now, is he?"

"Not yet, but wait until I show him the secret recipe I've got for him."

"Grams!"

The two of them quickly dissolved into a fit of laughter, Jordan shaking his head at just how explicit she was being. Clearly, she was on one. After they put away the muffins, Jordan helped her clean up some of the dishes. While he washed, she dried and stored them in the cabinets. They were a well-oiled machine.

It was times like these that reminded Jordan of just how

good he had it. It might not have been much to others, but these little things, like singing Teena Marie songs with his grandmother and cleaning up around the house, reminded him that he knew how to have fun outside of historical fiction and family sagas, Tony and Carla be damned, he thought.

By the time they were finished, it was nearly eleven, and Jordan unfortunately had to go. "Do you mind if I take a few of these with me?" he asked, gesturing to a plastic bowl filled with muffins. Sherleen waved her hand lazily.

"Take all you want, baby. My blood sugar's been pretty bad lately."

An ice bath of panic ran down the back of Jordan's neck. "Is everything alright?"

"Oh, I'm fine," she said with the same level of interest she'd given the muffins. "Nurse says I just need to watch what I eat. I say that old ugly bitch needs to mind her business."

"Grams, be nice," he warned. Jordan was relieved to hear that it was nothing serious. She was all he had left, and he didn't care if he had to eat every last sweet in the place or have a long, hard chat with this Powell man, he wasn't going to lose her too.

"You be nice," she said, rolling her eyes. "You heading out?"

"Yeah, I have to get ready for my book club."

"Oh yeah, Saturdays. How's that going, by the way?"

He shrugged with one shoulder. "Fine. There's this new guy..."

The mention of a man in Jordan's life was the flame to Sherleen's moth-like attention, and she turned to face him, an eager grin spreading across her face. Her brown eyes practically gleamed. "A man? What's his name?"

It was still strange, having these conversations with Sherleen. All her life, she'd used derogatory names and harped on his parents for not putting him in more "masculine" activities like sports. She'd grown up in a different time with different views, and though that wasn't an excuse, to her credit, she'd listened when he finally unloaded all of the internalized pain she'd caused him. It took years for her to not just wave off all her actions, but they were in a better place because of everything.

"I'd love to stay and chat, but..." Jordan tapped the watch he wasn't wearing and made his way to the door.

"Boy, if you don't get your narrow ass back—"

"Bye, Grams! Love you forever, I'll call you later tonight!" He closed the door behind him and hurried back to his car before she could grab her cane and chase after him. Not only did he avoid being hit, but he also avoided having the conversation about who or what Rex was to him.

On paper, they were nothing.

They were members of the same club. They read the same books. They occasionally sent each other memes at three in the morning and then pretended they didn't know each other after sunrise. It was nothing to write home about, and it was certainly not something Patricia Hayes or Jacquie Montgomery would ever find worthy of putting in their books.

Did his heartbeat suddenly skyrocket when Your New Favorite popped up on his screen? Maybe. Maybe mind your business, too.

Jordan knew not to expect much from this, deep down in his heart. He'd been around guys like Rex. They were fun for a while, but they never committed. Romantic nomads, bouncing from one guy's DMs to the next. He was just having fun. That was all.

Seriously.

Jordan made it home with thirty minutes left to spare before Meet Cute Club started. It was prep time. He ran all over the house, same as he did every weekend, perfecting the place and making it as welcoming as he could. While he fluffed all the pillows and laid out the prettiest muffins on the table, he fought back the self-doubt nagging in the back of his mind.

He wasn't sure how many more meetings they'd have,

and the act of not knowing always made him uncomfortable. Jordan *needed* to be in control, at all times, and with their membership slowly dwindling with every passing month, things weren't looking great.

Scolding himself, Jordan clenched his fists at his side. No. No more negativity. Even if he'd eventually have to put an end to all of this, he was going to enjoy the now. That's what life was about. Not living every day with one foot in tomorrow. He wanted to stand firmly in the moment.

As usual, Lana was first, strolling in with dragon queen-tier bleach blonde hair. Jordan nearly choked when he saw her.

"Oh my god," he exclaimed. "You look amazing."

Her saunter was exaggerated as she walked to the living room. "Decided to try a new hairstylist, and she convinced me to try a new look. Plus, now that it's blonde, I can dye it any color when I eventually get bored of all this."

Lana may not have been all that reliable, but Jordan admired her willingness to go with the flow and follow wherever her desires took her. For him, everything needed to be neat and pretty. If he lacked any kind of order, he found that his stress levels got even worse, and with high blood pressure running in his family, he made sure to keep his health a priority.

The meeting began at exactly noon. Jordan was surprised

to see that Rex had made it on time. He'd expected Rex to show up near the end of the meeting, not at all committed to actually being there. He ignored the urge to simply stare at Rex from across the room and stood up, starting off the meeting.

"Thanks for being here today, everyone!" he said, looking around the room at the other members. "I've been really excited to talk about *The Duke's Deadly Bride* all week."

"Me too!" Gloria said, nodding. "Jennifer really outdid herself on this one. I mean, that twist at the end? Probably the best thing I've read all year."

And so began the discussion of their latest book. Gloria went on and on about how well-paced this book was compared to Jennifer's last release, and Jordan had to agree that she had a point. *A Duel of Dukes* was steamier, but it didn't have the same kind of oomph that Jennifer's other books did. Madeline chimed in to say that it was nice seeing a Black character that wasn't treated terribly or just outright ignored.

As their conversations tripped over one another, Jordan couldn't help but notice how quiet Rex had been all afternoon. He'd nodded in agreement, but despite his love of getting on Jordan's nerves, he hadn't said much of anything.

"What about you, Rex? Did you like the book?"

"I did," he said, glancing at the others. "It's…kind of the first romance book I've read, so I have nothing to compare it to. It wasn't that bad, though."

Satisfaction warmed Jordan, and he smiled confidently. "Hey, 'not that bad' is a step up from the other things you said."

"I'm making progress," Rex replied facetiously. Despite his grumping and complaining, Jordan was pleased that he'd actually finished the book in its entirety. The man he'd met at Millerstone wouldn't have touched one of these books, let alone read it through.

When the conversation branched off and the members talked amongst themselves, Jordan rose from his seat and headed into the kitchen for refills. He had a hard time keeping the grin off his face as he brought out more muffins. This was what he needed. The stress of work and the impending doom that might fall upon Meet Cute Club had kept him from enjoying the good things he had going on for him.

"Do I get a gold sticker for finishing this thing?" Rex asked when Jordan took a seat across from him.

"Not until you do all your other chores, like taking out the trash and making your bed," Jordan replied coolly, though his words lacked any bite. He knew what Rex was doing, trying to distance himself from the fact that he'd read

Duke's.

"That hardly seems fair."

"I can pull an Elizabeth and tell you that men shouldn't be rewarded for doing what's required of them." Jordan raised an eyebrow, challenging him. One thing he'd loved about the book was how Elizabeth rarely took any of Hawthorne's shit.

"And do you remember what happened immediately after that scene, Jordan?"

Jordan flushed. He recalled desperately flying through those pages, devouring their love scene despite how innuendo-heavy and vague it had been. "I remember."

"So, if you're Elizabeth and I'm Hawthorne, that means—"

"Would you look at the time?" Lana said, glancing at her phone. "I've got to get out of here, but I'll text you guys later! Can't wait to start *Deadly Lovely Mine.*"

Charles nodded and said, "Yes! That one sounds really good."

Soon after Lana left, the others decided to head out as well. Jordan stood by the door, thanking each of the members for coming and wishing them a safe drive home. When he turned around, Rex stood in the living room with his gaze aimed right at him. Jordan swallowed hard.

"Are you...staying?"

"I thought I'd help clean up. No one else seemed to be offering, so…"

"That's nice of you," Jordan noted, taking a hesitant step towards him. "You really don't have to, though. I do this by myself all the time, anyway."

"That's because I wasn't a member of Meet Cute Club before. Now I am."

Jordan tried his best to keep his expression neutral, because inside, he was having a minor freak out. What was Rex's game plan here? Did he truly just want to help out, without any caveats or ulterior motives?

"Okay," Jordan said. "You can help me clean up all these bottles and the cupcake liners if you want."

"Sure."

They worked at opposite ends of the living room, grabbing various bottles of water, glasses of tea, and other small pieces of trash that had been left around by the other members. Jordan reached for a balled-up cupcake liner just as Rex did, and he wanted to die on the spot.

How absolutely painfully cliché was this?

Jordan pulled his hand back quickly, muttering a brief, "I'm sorry."

Cool as ever, Rex chuckled and grabbed the trash. "Don't be, handsome."

Before he could spontaneously combust and paint his

61

white walls red, Jordan carried his haul of garbage to the kitchen, where he dumped it all in the bin and washed his hands. Rex was right behind him a moment later.

As he ran his hands beneath the faucet, Rex said, "I read that other book you recommended, too. The Patricia Hayes one."

"Yeah?" It didn't matter who it was; Jordan always got giddy when people said they read the books he'd suggested. "What'd you think about it?"

"Much better than *Duke's*. There was no obnoxious grand apology with a dozen hand-picked roses or anything, so right off the bat, that makes it ten times better. You were right about me liking it more."

"See?" Jordan smirked. "I told you it was good. Have I turned you into a fan yet?"

Rex reached for a paper towel to dry off his hands. "Not even close," he said. "I may need some more convincing to stay in the club."

"If all these muffins and drinks didn't convince you, nothing will."

"No, I can think of some things that might." Rex took another step towards him, dragging his fingers over the dining table.

Jordan was willing to play this game. "What kind of things?"

"I've always been convinced by a nice pair of lips."

It was a fairly effective line, but Jordan wasn't going to let him off the hook that easily. He took the next step, only a foot away from the other man. "Where in the world could we find a pair of those?"

"You seem to be in possession of two perfectly good ones."

"So I am," Jordan murmured.

Rex closed the gap between them, his broad chest practically pressing against Jordan's. He wore the worst, most mischievous grin Jordan had ever seen, and he wanted desperately to knock it off his face. To catch this cocky bastard off guard and show him that he wasn't as in control as he always assumed he was.

Whatever came over him, Jordan couldn't explain. The heat of the moment, or maybe some underlying desire to show Rex he wasn't the only one with confidence. No matter the explanation, it led to the same result.

Jordan reached a tentative hand up and cupped the side of Rex's stubbled chin, dragging his fingertips over the bristles.

"Are you going to kiss me and convince me to stay?" Rex asked.

"No."

Rex blinked. "Why not?"

"Because *you're* going to kiss me. You'll lift me up and set me on the counter and kiss me until you feel lightheaded. And when you're done, you'll say thank you and tell me that you're committed to this club."

Jordan waited, momentarily afraid that he'd been too forward. He'd fought too hard to take the steering wheel, and now, they were careening off the freeway.

Rex put those doubts to rest when he grabbed Jordan's behind and hefted him, dropping him on the counter gracelessly. He took Jordan's face in his hands and studied him, stroking over his bottom lip with his thumb. As he inched his finger closer, Jordan nipped at it.

"Kiss me," Jordan whispered.

"You're so damn bossy," Rex muttered. Without hesitation, he leaned forward and pressed his lips to Jordan's.

For the briefest moment, it was completely wrong.

Too much tongue, not enough lips, and an awkward exchanging of breath. The moment the two found their groove, it suddenly clicked. Jordan turned his head just slightly, parting his lips to graciously welcome Rex inside. He dragged his hands up the ridges of his arms, the sensation better than any daydream could ever possibly simulate.

Rex's beard scratched him, but it was a pleasant contrast

to the softness of his mouth. Rex was an expert, skilled with his tongue in a way that sent a new wave of electric pleasure through Jordan every few seconds. He moaned against the man's lips and wrapped his legs around his hips, and when their bodies fit together like a lock and its key, any doubt that this wasn't exactly what Jordan wanted disappeared completely.

He stroked Rex's tongue with his own, greedy for the faint taste of cranberry and the warm, wet heat that made every hair on his arms stand at full, erect attention. He didn't care if he looked ugly or how ragged their breathing had become. Not with Rex's arms around his waist and his forehead pressed against Jordan's.

He forced himself back, lightheaded and unsure whether any of this was real. He opened his eyes slowly to find Rex dipping his head and attacking his neck with the same enthusiastic kisses.

That beard and that mouth. Jordan couldn't help but picture taking a seat on both of them and letting his filthiest desires run free. The trouble he and Rex could get into... Those thoughts drove him to tighten the hold of his legs and grind his hips forward, allowing Rex to feel just how well-received this all was. The aching friction between them elicited another moan, and Jordan couldn't determine whether it was Rex's or his own.

Rex's lips moved along the line of his jaw, and when he reached the curve of his ear, he lightly bit down. "Someone's excited." His voice was molasses thick, and Jordan's stomach clenched at the sound.

"Two someones, I'd say," he replied. He rolled his hips for added emphasis. Just beyond the fabric of Rex's jeans, Jordan knew he'd find the same throb of excitement.

Rex began to speak again when a frantic knock came from the living room. In an instant, Jordan freed Rex from the vice trap of his legs and hopped down, adjusting himself. He hurried to the front door to find Charles bashfully smiling.

"Hey, Charles, what's up?" He felt out of breath, like he'd just run a marathon. Charles picked up on something immediately, suspicion darkening his face. Jordan put on a plastic smile.

"Sorry to disturb you," the man said, his eyes cutting to Rex in the living room. Rex waved. "I forgot my book over by the sofa. I got halfway home before I remembered I'd set it down."

Jordan nodded and stepped aside. "Come in, please."

"It'll just be a second," the older man replied. He bent over the couch and produced a small paperback. "Gotcha. Thanks, Jordan. Bye, Rex."

"Later, Charles!" Rex called, hands in his back pocket

and his lips pressed into a tight line.

When Jordan shut the door, he closed his eyes and shook his head. What they were doing wasn't against any specific rules, but it still felt like he'd been caught with his pants down.

Rex was at his side a moment later. "I should get out of here. Got some homework to do for the next meeting."

Jordan nodded. "Sure, sure. I'll, uh… I'll text you tonight?"

"Send me nudes."

"Get out of my house." Jordan swung open the door and pushed Rex past the threshold, fighting back the urge to join him in his laughter.

At the curb, Rex swung a leg over his motorcycle and turned to face Jordan. "I'm serious. Dirty pictures, right on my phone. Tonight."

"Rex, I don't say this often, but I'm going to kick your ass," Jordan said with a grin.

"Mm, you promise?"

Jordan huffed and rolled his eyes, stomping back to the front door. He could just barely make out that Rex Bailey cackle before he slammed the door shut. In the privacy of his own home, he finally let his ear-to-ear grin free.

Five

If mornings were alcoholic beverages, Jordan would've considered this one a nice hot glass of cheap beer. He'd been on the phone since eight talking to his bosses, trying to work out their disagreement about his potential raise without losing his cool. Was it too much to ask for that he get paid for additional work?

The worst part was that no matter who he talked to, they all seemed to be fighting their hardest to talk him down. All the bogus excuses were grating on his patience, and before he could lose his shit entirely, he simply told John—one of the least terrible executives at the company—that he was done having this discussion.

"John, with all due respect, I can't keep going in circles with you guys. I'm not asking to be promoted to a manager.

I don't want that, and I know you don't have room for another one. I just want you to work with me. I'm saving you money from having to hire another employee. Kicking me a raise isn't an absurd request."

He was proud of himself for keeping his voice as level as he could. He'd practically smashed the banana he was eating between his fist, but from the sound of it, he was as calm as could be. He wasn't stupid. Sherleen had taught him long ago to never let them take him there. It wasn't until he'd started working that he realized who "they" were.

"Jordan, listen, buddy. I want to help you. I understand that you're frustrated, but right now, it's just not in the budget."

"But I think it is."

"And I'm telling you it's not."

Jordan grit his teeth and said, "It's not my job."

There was a long silence, and under normal circumstances, he would've been uneasy about the quiet. At the moment, though, all he wanted to do was watch the world burn to ash. Which was why when John replied with, "I'm sorry, but it is," he snapped back with,

"It's not in my job description, and I'm not going to do this anymore."

"Is this you quitting, Jordan?"

His heart thudded up into his throat, and the shrill,

rational voice in the back of his head screamed itself silly trying to warn him to back down. Back down and just take it. Take it, deal with it, work through it.

"Yeah, John, it is. I'm not doing work I'm not getting paid for. Now you'll have to fill another position."

"Alright. I'll let Martin know that you've made your decision."

"Great. Have a wonderful morning, and tell Martin I said thank you for the opportunity." Sarcasm spilled from his lips like tar, and he hung up the phone before he could say anything else reckless. That was when the realization of what he'd just done sank in.

"What the fuck?" he breathed, clutching his shirt. He'd really just done that. All those weeks fantasizing about quitting his dead-end job, and he'd *really* just done it. Immediately, he felt sick to his stomach. He was unemployed.

Bills. Rent. The cost of living.

Everything hit him at once, over and over, and for a minute, he was sure he was going to pass out. Jordan's chest tightened and his stomach twisted, all the telltale signs that one of his anxiety attacks was on the brink.

But he had Meet Cute Club happening shortly, and he couldn't lose his shit before their meeting. He had to keep it together. Regain control.

Breathe.

Jordan closed his eyes and inhaled through his belly, centering himself to keep from exploding all over the kitchen. He reminded himself of his savings. Since he'd started working at the call center, he'd kept money in his rainy-day fund. Enough to live off of for at least six months. He would find a job before that money ran out. He would be fine. He'd planned for a situation like this.

Eventually, the swell of panic settled, and he was able to think clearly once more.

It took a few moments to stand up straighter, but Jordan forced himself to continue on with his morning. He still had company coming over, and he owed it to them to keep the same level of energy he always provided.

After a quick trip to the grocery store (and some time perusing the new arrivals in the romance section), Jordan returned home with two bags full of groceries. Whenever he needed an escape from the tornado of thoughts in his head, he tried out a new recipe. With all his focus on not screwing up the hors d'oeuvres, it was easy to put aside his stress and calm down.

The snack for this meeting was a cheese bread recipe he'd found while scrolling through Pinterest. He knew that none of his members had any specific allergies and figured they might be sick of all the constant sweets he pumped everyone full of. It would be a nice change of pace.

Bouncing around the kitchen, the last of Jordan's anxiety finally disappeared, and he was able to put a smile on once more. With everything he'd gone through in his life, from his parents' deaths to his struggle with his sexuality, he'd learned that sitting and simmering in one place did no good. It might've even been unhealthy, though he had no scientific evidence to back up that claim.

Whenever he found himself facing a tough situation, he had to be active. Proactive, even. That was why, when he popped the loaf of bread from the tin and plated it, he gave himself a pat on the back. He could've just as easily fallen to the kitchen floor in one of his worst panic attacks in a long time. But he didn't. He'd made *this* beautiful creation.

Things were going to turn around for him, and if they didn't, he was going to turn them around all on his own.

With a quick change of clothes, he returned to the living room in a pair of jeans and his favorite black and white striped hoodie. He'd picked it up on his way to a book signing after the person beside him on the bus spilled her coffee down the side of his previous favorite hoodie. There'd been a small boutique not too far from the bookstore, and he was able to save the day from disaster with a simple thirty-five-dollar purchase.

As usual, Lana showed up at his front door first, and just

as unsurprisingly, she had new hair. Gone was the platinum blonde, this time replaced with a red color vibrant enough to make little mermaids jealous.

"Every time I see you, Lana," he said, shaking his head and giving her a quick hug.

"Variety is the spice of life, baby."

While they waited for the others to arrive, Jordan and Lana talked about what she'd been up to in the past week. Lana gushed about some foreign movie she'd gone to the theater to see, and how it changed her life forever. He tried to get the name of the film from her, but her attention span moved like a rabbit, from one topic to the next without any hesitation or sign of slowing down.

For as fast as she talked, Jordan noticed the way she rerouted every conversation away from Meet Cute Club. When he brought up the book, she laughed and started on another story about something that had happened to her downtown last weekend. She'd even admitted to forgetting her copy at home. He wasn't normally a suspicious person, but all of his alarms were going off.

Something was up with her.

The knocks at the door were her chance to escape. Lana hopped up and hurried to greet the other members, starting brand new conversations with all of them. Jordan figured he'd let it go for the time being, but as soon as the meeting was over and they'd all raved over *Deadly Lovely Mine*, he found himself buzzing around her, quietly trying to piece together why her energy felt off.

"Hey," he said in a hushed voice. Around him, the other members stood chatting about their families and the next book they were reading. To his surprise, even Rex was in the middle of a discussion about the book for the following week.

"Hey, Jordan, I was actually wondering if I could talk to you for a minute?" Lana pulled him aside, away from the chatter, and lowered her voice as well. "Listen, please don't be mad at me, but I think this might be my last day of Meet Cute Club."

It was like being hit with a bag of sand. Jordan blinked, momentarily certain that he'd heard her incorrectly. Lana wasn't leaving. She was just messing with him. From the uneasy smile she gave him, Jordan knew his face revealed every thought in his mind.

"I'm sorry," she said, frowning. "I just have so much on my plate right now. I'm actually going to start this pottery club with my mom. At first, I thought it was kind of silly, but she's really convinced me, and I can't say no to her. She's been feeling better lately, but the doctors are still worried she might not stay in remission for very long."

Jordan's first impulse was to be upset with Lana, but he

knew that would be unfair. With the fight Lana's mother had been through and how hard she worked to get better, she deserved to spend time with her daughter. It stung, but he wasn't a monster.

"I…I'm okay. I think you should do it. Your mom is more important, of course. Please don't feel bad, okay?"

A look of relief washed across Lana's face, and she nodded. "Thank you. I promise, it won't be forever, either. If something changes, I'll be right back here, okay?"

"Sure, sure. And tell your mom that I'm glad she's feeling better."

"Definitely!"

Lana made rounds in the room to say goodbye to everyone, then disappeared outside. Following suit, it didn't take the other members more than a few minutes to pack up and say their goodbyes. Rex sat on the sofa silently, but Jordan couldn't bring himself to look at the man for very long. Too many thoughts raced around his mind for him to focus on Rex as well.

Jordan made quick work of cleaning, grabbing a bag and tossing paper plates inside of it.

"Let me help you clean," Rex offered, rising from his seat and sticking a hand out for the bag Jordan was holding.

"I got it."

"Seriously," Rex said, reaching out again. This time,

Jordan took a step back.

"I said I got it. I don't need your help right now, okay?"

Momentarily stunned, Rex could only watch as Jordan moved around the living room picking up trash. He considered leaving the conversation right then and there. Whatever was on his mind was heavy, and Jordan struck him as the type that needed to be alone to process his feelings. At the same time, it wouldn't feel right to just leave him here when something was so obviously bothering him.

"What's wrong?" he asked, crossing his arms over his chest. "You were weird during the meeting today, and you're being weird right now. What happened? Is it something Lana said?"

Jordan's eyes snapped up. "Did you overhear our conversation?"

"No. I just saw how upset you looked at the end of it. Is everything okay?"

"Not really. Lana told me that this meeting was her last. She's getting into pottery now, and she won't have time for both activities." He tossed garbage into his bag with a little more force than before. "And I'm not mad at her. She's allowed to leave if she wants. But people *keep* leaving. I thought when you joined, we'd be on an upward swing, but that's not what's happening. We gained a new member and lost an old one. We're exactly where we started."

For the first time in a while, Rex didn't know how to respond. This was out of his wheelhouse. Whenever Amy came to him with her disappointments, he always found a way to cheer her up through sarcasm or humor, but this wasn't the same. He didn't know Jordan the same way. He was starting to get a better picture of the man, sure, but there were still integral parts of him that were a mystery.

Rather than his tried and true method of a joke, Rex said, "I'm sorry Lana's leaving. But that doesn't mean the club is ending. There are still four of us that want to do this with you. It's not a competition."

"It's not," Jordan said, desperation in his voice, "but my grandma would've never had this problem. She didn't. She knew how to run things like this."

"What?"

Sighing, Jordan collapsed on the sofa across from Rex. "When I was little, she'd always take me to her book club meetings. Some of my oldest memories are of listening to her read passages from books, or all of her friends giggling about some cute waiter at the restaurant they always held their meetings at. She made it look easy. Everyone loved being together and just fangirling over whatever they were reading. Nobody ever dropped out. Nobody ever lost interest. And all I keep doing is losing members. I try to be on her level, and I just…can't."

It was the break in Jordan's voice, just barely decipherable, that gave Rex all the information he needed. This wasn't just something fun to do on the weekends to avoid thinking about the failing economy and the state of the government. This wasn't Jordan's self-medication the way it might be to so many others.

He cared about this. The kind of care that could drive a person to act irrationally, to end up nearly in tears over a harmless hobby. For whatever reason—and try as he might to fight it—Rex felt his Grinch-sized heart squeeze at the sight of Jordan's wide brown eyes cutting across the room, a sparkle of tears just on his red-rimmed lashes.

"Hey," he said, his voice unexpectedly soft.

It took a moment, but finally, Jordan looked back at him. "What?"

"It's gonna be okay, man. You don't have to get this upset, okay?"

In a flash, his sadness turned to contempt. "You don't understand, Rex. I don't expect you to. I'm sure to you, I look like a child sitting here crying over this. If that's what you want to think, then fine. I don't give a fuck, okay?"

With palms open to signal his innocence, Rex said, "Jordan, I'm not making fun of you. I get it. This club matters to you. More than anyone else. You'd never want to see something you care about fail. And I promise, I'm not making fun of you for caring. It's…"

"It's what?"

"It's kind of cool."

Jordan scoffed. "Yeah, okay."

"I mean it. Do you know how many people would kill to have the same kind of passion as you? There are people who don't even care about their kids as much as you care about Meet Cute Club. That *says* something. I would never make fun of you for loving something that much."

Though his face softened, Jordan's words were still sharp, a knife dragging just along the line of Rex's pulsing neck. "I know the kind of guy you are, Rex. You like to make fun of people because you like getting under their skin. Don't think I'm gullible enough to fall for this nice guy act all of a sudden."

Despite his sincerity, Rex smirked. "I do like getting under your skin, sure. But I'm serious. Meet Cute Club is gonna be fine."

"You don't know that," Jordan said. He stood from the couch and turned his back, wiping his eyes before he began picking up the small mess in the living room. "People are dropping like flies around here. By the end of the year, I'm sure it'll just be me and one other member."

"You really doubt me that much?"

"What?"

"I told you this club is going to be fine, because I'm here. I'm going to help you with it. And I don't lose."

Rex watched Jordan's body stiffen. With a snail's pace, he turned to look at Rex once more. His suspicion couldn't have been more obvious if he said it out loud. "Why are you going to help me? You don't really care about this club. You just want to bother me."

"That's not true," Rex said, his voice rising an octave. "Maybe I don't love it as much as you, but it's pretty, y'know…cool. I guess."

"You guess."

Rex hopped from the couch and reached out to Jordan, grabbing his forearms and staring him down. "Jordan, I'm going to help you with this, do you hear me? I may be an asshole, and kind of a douchebag—"

"And obnoxious, and irritatingly persistent—"

"And an amazing kisser that practically left you panting on the kitchen counter, yes, yes, we know. But beyond all that, I'm not heartless. I don't look at someone in need of help and ignore them. So, I'm going to make you a promise. You give me a chance, and we'll make this club the best damn thing in Sweet Rose. People will be lined up to join. You might even have to rent somewhere else to host your meetings."

That was the magic mental image. Rex could see it in the

way Jordan's eyes glazed over and his smile grew dreamy, visualizing hordes of people just as eager to dive into the latest Angelica Whoever's novel. For the briefest moment, Rex's heart did that same annoying double-thud, but he squashed the emotion beneath his boot, reminding himself that this was all fun. Hope only led to misery, and for the first time in his life, he was done being miserable.

He was going to focus on the present, and presently, his goal was to cheer Jordan up and make his book club better than it had ever been before.

"Don't screw with me, Rex. You said it yourself, I love this club more than a child. Do you know what parents do when someone messes with their child?"

Rex was willing to bet his life's savings—however small—on the fact that Jordan meant every last word of his threat. As adorably uptight as the man was, he'd seen his fair share of documentary series on the ID Channel. He knew how easily people could flip the switch. He also knew that if he spent any more time imagining Jordan's perfect face scrunched up in indignant rage, he might end up turning himself on.

"I'm not screwing with you, Jordan, Jesus Christ."

"Watch it," Jordan warned, and Rex was once again reminded just how close to a Southern belle this guy was, all prim and proper and shit.

"Do you want my help or not, man? Take me or leave me."

Jordan's eyes narrowed for a moment, deep in thought, until he finally said, "I'll take you."

"I'm sure you could."

"Behave."

Rex chuckled out a half-hearted, "Sorry, low-hanging fruit."

"We have work to do. If we're gonna make this club the next big thing, we need to get the word out. You think you can handle that, Rex?"

Feigning insult, Rex donned an exaggerated Okie accent to say, "You think I don't know how to get attention? Why, I never…"

Jordan's head fell back as he groaned, stomping off to the kitchen to throw away the trash in his hands. "Kill me now, God."

Rex would've normally found himself rolling his eyes at just how dramatic Jordan could be, but his gaze was glued to the man's ass as he walked away. He didn't consider himself all that religious, but a gift like the one Jordan walked around with was the only evidence he needed for divine creation.

Six

"You take any longer to dial that phone number and I'm going to do it myself," Amy warned Rex, putting one hand up on her hip and narrowing her eyes at him.

"Yeah, right," he muttered, turning around and staring down at his phone. What the hell was wrong with him? He'd asked a million and one guys out before, and none of them ever made him feel this anxious. This was the furthest from how he operated, and the fact that he was twisting himself in knots over how to approach the situation frustrated him more than anything else had.

Jordan struck him as the wary type, always triple-checking before he leapt, and Rex wasn't sure if his typical laissez-faire technique would garner the same positive results it usually did. Jordan might just laugh him off and tell him they'd see each other at the next Meet Cute Club meeting.

Before he could make his decision, Amy suddenly snatched the phone from him and pressed CALL, smirking at him and waving the phone in his face. "Amy, give me the damn phone!"

She spun around, avoiding his hand thrusting towards her for his cellphone. When he tried again, she let out a laugh and dashed to the other side of the room.

"I swear to god, Amy," he warned. She dodged one more lunge before turning around and tossing it at his chest.

"I told you I would," she said, winking at him. Rex had half a mind to throw one of Nana Bailey's dusty couch pillows at her, but just as the thought popped into his mind, he heard Jordan's voice on the other end of the line.

"Hello? Rex?"

Clearing his throat and straightening up, he said, "Hey. I didn't interrupt your precious reading time, did I?"

"No. Just my precious Not Talking to Rex time. What's up?"

Rex cracked a smile at the insult. "I was wondering if you were busy later today. I'm off for the day, and I had an idea." With how laid-back his boss Carla was at Millerstone, Rex's hours were constantly shifting, giving them all day to hang out.

"Wow, a whole idea all on your own?"

"You're especially snippy today, aren't you? Seriously, are you doing anything?"

"No. What did you want to do?"

This was the part Rex had been anticipating all morning, ever since he'd made up the decision that he was actually going to ask Jordan out rather than only see him when they had their meetings for the club. Seeing Jordan in his element was always nice, but he was tired of having to split his time with five other people. Well, four now.

"I was thinking we could head over to somewhere pretty damn special to me. You don't have to come if you don't want to, but I think you'd really enjoy it."

The curiosity in Jordan's voice was palpable. "Where would we be going?"

"I can't ruin the surprise now, can I?"

Across the room, Amy gave him an exaggerated eye roll and stuck her finger down her throat. This time, Rex did manage to snag one of the pillows from the loveseat and hit her right in the face with it. She burst out laughing and quickly straightened her hair in the mirror.

"If you have a date with a good Christian cowboy and his Southern belle love interest, that's totally fine," Rex continued. He was absolutely baiting Jordan, and something inside him said it was going to work hook, line, and sinker.

"I'm not busy. You can pick me up at two."

"One."

"Fine. I'll see you then." And with that, the line went dead. Rex hated how wide his smile was, and he forced himself to cough so he had a reason to cover his mouth. It was all in vain, however, because the moment Amy spotted that toothy grin, she went in for the kill.

"Rhett, you're positively *blushing* right now."

"Fuck off, no, I am not."

"Rhett's got a boyfriend, Rhett's got a boyfriend!" When she stopped her teasing, she returned the pillow to the loveseat and said, "You really like this guy, don't you?"

His first instinct was to deny, deny, deny. No one ever got this power over him. No one ever got to take him to this level, to the point where he was feeling all mushy on the inside. He'd always made it a point to have that power, to be the crusher, not the crushee, yet Jordan had somehow turned the tables on him in a way that simultaneously intrigued and infuriated him.

"He's fine," Rex managed to say casually. Amy gave him a *look*, but he didn't care. He wasn't going to admit that there might've been a chance he wanted to spend more time with Jordan to himself, let alone his obnoxious kid sister. She'd have a fucking field day with it, and he refused to let her have that much leverage.

"Sure. Just know that whenever you two get married, I want to be your best woman. I also plan to find the love of my life at your wedding, too. Maybe a groomsman will sweep me off my feet…"

Rex snorted. "You sure you don't want to join Meet Cute Club? You'd fit right in with all the other hopeless romantics."

"I'd only be getting my hopes up," Amy sighed. "My love life is more Shakespeare than Alyssa Cole. But you and your boyfriend have fun."

"He's not my boyfriend, brat," Rex grumbled, but it was already too late. Amy had latched onto the nickname, and he was never going to get her to stop referring to Jordan that way. Rather than dwelling on the inevitable jeering his younger sister would do, he threw himself into cleaning out the rest of the room, attempting to ignore the tiny little spark of excitement stirring in the pit of his stomach.

Jordan paced back and forth in his room like he was trying to compete with his Roomba, unable to sit still for more than a few minutes before his nerves lit up all over again. He wasn't nervous, but he also wasn't sure if this situation was entirely platonic.

Sure, he and Rex talked sometimes, trading funny pictures and giving each other occasional updates on the books they were reading, but this wasn't just meeting up at his house with everyone else. They'd be alone, wherever Rex planned on taking him, and as someone that needed to know where he was going and who all would be there, Jordan was losing his cool piece by piece.

He'd changed his outfit three times, finally settling on a baggy sweater and jeans, but with how long it was taking Rex to text him and let him know he was outside, Jordan reconsidered his clothing choice once again. He had to discipline himself and put his foot down. It didn't matter what he was wearing, because this wasn't a date, because making out with Rex in his kitchen a few weeks ago didn't mean anything.

People kissed all the time.

People kissed others they had no real interest in all the time.

People kissed and dry humped each other like it was going out of season all the time.

Okay, so maybe there *was* something there. Maybe this *was* a date. That thought only sent Jordan up into another tizzy, but graciously, his phone vibrated to let him know that there was no time to panic. Rex was outside.

He took a quick, controlled breath before heading downstairs and out to the curb. He found Rex leaning against his motorcycle, helmet under his arm like he was posing for the cover of People. He wore a long-sleeved heather grey Henley, dark wash distressed jeans, and a pair of boots that looked as if they'd seen better days. It all worked for Rex, however, and Jordan could've easily stared for much longer had time allowed for it.

"This is…" Jordan started, gesturing to the motorcycle. "We're taking this?"

"Yes, sir. You're not scared, are you?"

He could hear the underlying snark in Rex's tone, but in a moment of honesty, he simply said, "Yeah, a little…"

"Don't be. I've only been in nine accidents. Everyone knows you get ten free before you should start to worry." Jordan gave a weak smile, but he couldn't feign bravery as well as he'd have liked. Rex handed over his helmet. "I brought this for you. If you're not into it, I can just order us a car or something. It's up to you."

Oddly enough, Rex had immediately dropped all his sarcasm and wit. He stared at Jordan, watching and waiting for his reaction. "No," Jordan said, taking the helmet and pulling it over his head. "This is okay. I'm okay."

"You sure?"

"Yeah, I'll be alright. I trust you not to smear us across the road."

"That's the sweetest thing anyone's ever said to me," Rex replied. He raised his eyebrows twice, then swung a leg over the bike. Jordan followed suit, scooting close enough to press his chest to the other's back.

"So, I just hang on like this?" he asked, getting comfortable with his arms around Rex's chest. Momentarily, he worried that Rex could feel his pounding heartbeat with their bodies this close together, but rationality won. When the bike roared to life, Rex wouldn't be able to feel anything but the purr of his ride.

"Just like that. Keep your thighs tight, too. And if you need me to pull over or stop for a second, just let me know, alright?"

Still uneasy about his kindness, Jordan pressed closer to the man and nodded. "Sure."

Through sheer concentration and his determination not to chicken out, Jordan was able to keep from flinching or squeezing Rex too tight the moment they pulled away from the curb. He could tell by the speed that they started with that Rex was giving him time to adjust, and that only made it easier for him to finally open his eyes and look around.

He'd driven around Sweet Rose for just over a decade, and because of that experience, he thought he knew what his tiny Oklahoma town looked like. Riding forty miles an hour on the back of a bike proved just how wrong he was. The spring flowers looked even brighter, the nearby restaurants smelled even better, and with the wind whipping in his face and his stomach practically sinking down into his toes, he let out an almost maniacal laugh. This wasn't that bad. In fact, as they turned right onto Addleston Road, Jordan found himself never wanting this to end.

"You having fun?" Rex called out, his stomach contracting beneath Jordan's arms as he laughed.

"Hell yes," Jordan shouted back.

Much to his disappointment, the ride ended five minutes later when Rex came to a halt outside of a building Jordan had never been to. He recognized it from the name— Riverside Library—and immediately, he was curious why they'd come here of all places.

As if reading his mind, Rex stepped off the bike and said, "Welcome to my second home." Rex took the helmet from Jordan and squatted to lock it to his motorcycle before he continued. "My parents weren't the best at the whole marriage thing. Lots of fighting, actually. Whenever things ended up too bad, I'd grab my little Huffy and pedal all the way out here for some peace and quiet. Ended up becoming best friends with all the librarians."

Rex led the way through the double doors of the building, and Jordan followed close behind, looking around at one of the murals the neighborhood kids had all pitched in to create. He immediately recognized covers of some of the most notable children's books in the business, each of them drawn by a child.

"At first, I mostly just stopped by to use the free internet. Back in the day, they even had a few games installed that I messed around with. Finally, one afternoon my favorite librarian Mr. Diaz came up to me and told me that I wasn't allowed to sit on the computer all day. For every hour I played games, I had to read something. When I tell you I was pissed off…"

Jordan laughed at the idea of a tiny Rex Bailey glaring up at an authority figure. "What'd you do? Tell him off or something?"

"Believe it or not, no. I was mad, but I also would've rather spent every day here reading than another second at home. So, I told him to show me the best books and I'd consider it. He brought me to the shelf where they kept all the favorites."

"What'd you read? Something like *Harry Potter*?"

"I read those, sure, but I had a secret favorite series that no one else knew about." The smile on Rex's face was just as mischievous as Jordan imagined he might wear when the man was younger. Conspiratorial, but so self-satisfied at the same time.

Jordan couldn't help but grin as well. "What was it?"

"*Sweet Valley High.*"

"Bullshit," Jordan said without thinking. He covered his

mouth and looked around, immediately relieved that there weren't any children around that could've overheard him. "You're lying," he insisted.

"No lie." Rex took Jordan by the hand and led him through the stick-covered archway leading into the children's section. An older Latino man sitting behind the counter looked up at him, and recognition crossed his face instantly.

"Is that little Rhett Bailey?" he demanded, his voice husky and booming.

"Yes, sir," he said.

"You remember what I told you?" Mr. Diaz narrowed his eyes at Rex with faux severity.

Rex nodded almost obediently. "One hour of books, one hour of games. I sure do. Also, by any chance, do you still have those books I used to read? You know…the ones I didn't want anyone else to know about?"

"Something tells me we might have one or two somewhere in here. We got rid of most of them when we updated a few years ago. Let me see…" The man rose from his chair, straightened out his argyle sweater over his round belly, and disappeared behind a shelf of books in the back of the room. A moment later, he returned with a copy of *On the Edge*. "This work for you?"

"This is perfect, thanks, Mr. Diaz." Rex led Jordan to a

small alcove in the back of the room, hidden from view. He took a seat in one of the armchairs and flipped through the weathered paperback until he got to the right page. "Aha," he said, turning it around for Jordan to see.

Written in green pen at the bottom of one of the pages were the initials "R.B." in handwriting that could only belong to a child.

Jordan traced his finger over the letters and smiled softly. "You know this is adorable, right? Like, almost too cute for me to believe that this was you?"

"We all have our dark pasts, JJ."

Jordan cocked his head inquisitively. "JJ?"

"Do you hate it?"

After a moment of consideration, Jordan said, "Not at all."

"Good." Rex reached over to take the book back, flipping through it absently. "If I remember correctly, this is the first book in the series where things get very after-school special. The protagonist in this one does one bump of coke and straight up dies. Maybe not the best thing for me to be reading at nine, but it was far from the craziest shit that happened in this series."

"And this was for kids?"

"Technically, it was for young adults, but... And in Francine's defense, this was tamer than the following books.

I haven't even gotten to the girl that killed her foster sister and an old lady to pretend to be one of the twins, or when the girls thought there was a real-life werewolf in London killing people…"

Utterly fascinated with the mildly unhinged storylines of the series, Jordan got comfortable in the armchair facing Rex, smiling and nodding as the man went into great detail about the entire six-part miniseries leading to the 100th book or the three-part miniseries about the girls studying in England. He'd never seen Rex this animated before, and in the back of his mind, he had to wonder if this was what he looked like when he talked about Patricia Hayes. Did his eyes go wide like that? Did he move his arms around that much?

At the beginning of the afternoon, Jordan had wondered why Rex brought him to the Riverside library. For a moment, he'd worried he was bringing him here to tease him and show him "good" books, the same way he might have when they first met at Millerstone. But the more Rex went into detail, reading from *On the Edge* and other books he hopped up to collect, it was clear that this was Rex's way of sharing his own love of stories with him.

For the first time, Rex dropped all pretenses and seemed to just be letting himself have fun, and despite the way he'd been left breathless in the kitchen after their first kiss,

Jordan felt his heart race even more now.

"Why are you looking at me like that?" Rex asked suspiciously, his mouth tugged into a lopsided smile that showed his slightly crooked teeth.

"No reason."

"Bull—" He caught himself. "BS."

"No BS," Jordan insisted. "It's just that I've never seen you be this excited before. About anything."

Rex sat back in his chair and shrugged. "It's no big deal."

"It is a big deal. I think it's really cool that you get this interested in these books. It's actually really dang cute, too." Cute was probably the last word he'd ever have used to describe Rex, with his rugged appearance and the aura of a troublemaker practically pulsating around him. Sexy, sure. Maybe even *fine*. But not cute.

Yet here he was, ready to reach over, pinch his cheeks, and call him a "wittle baby."

"I'm not cute. You're cute," Rex said, muttering his compliment. "Are you having fun, though? I hope I'm not boring you too much."

"Not at all. I can't wait until you start talking about all the young adult books you read."

Rex's eyes went wide again. "Those are upstairs. C'mon, I'll show you."

Like before, he took Jordan's hand in his, lacing their

fingers together, and led him up the grand staircase in the middle of the first floor. Jordan almost couldn't believe how excited he was to learn more about Rex, but in this moment, nothing mattered more than walking down memory lane with the man, hand in hand and wearing the widest, cheesiest smile he'd put on in weeks.

Seven

Jordan was starting to think that surprise trips were Rex's thing. After their date to the library last week, Rex had insisted that he take Jordan somewhere else, and just like before, he refused to tell him anything about their destination. Even when Jordan begged and pleaded over the phone, Rex's lips were tight.

"Just one hint?" Jordan asked as he climbed onto the back of Rex's motorcycle.

"No hints, stop asking. I promise you'll like it, alright?"

"Fine." Jordan's dejection was over the minute Rex revved up his engine and pulled away from the curb. Immediately, he was hit with the same rush of adrenaline that left him giddy with excitement. Even better, the ride took longer than before, giving Jordan time to admire Sweet

Rose for just a bit longer.

At the stop light on Main Street, he turned his head to watch the Donovan Activity Center fill with people from all over town, some of them sporting workout clothes while other artsier types walked around with bags full of painting supplies. He'd only been to the building once before, for a birthday party when he was younger, but from what he remembered, it was a nice place to meet up with friends and become more social.

With all the free time he had after quitting his job, maybe it wouldn't hurt to stop by sometime.

The thought of being unemployed still filled Jordan with existential dread, but Rex had become quite the distraction. They'd started talking on the phone even more, skipping texts altogether. Groundbreaking it wasn't, but with how call-averse Jordan and his generation seemed to be, it felt like it held more weight than a simple Snapchat message.

Rex and Jordan sped off when the light turned green, and Jordan closed his eyes tight, dropping his chin on Rex's shoulder. When he inhaled, he was greeted with the smell of citrus and something earthy and masculine. Just beneath all that, he could detect the lavender soap Rex used to wash his clothes.

The combination all added up to Rex, and Jordan wasn't sure whether he'd ever smelled anything as nice, and warm, and inviting.

Rex cut the engine outside of a small suburban house with a lawn clearly in need of a bit of TLC. A large pink tricycle lay overturned near the driveway, and various other toys scattered the path up to the front door. Rex led the way, knocking a few times before he looked back at Jordan.

"Now, don't be scared when you see him, okay?" he warned, and like clockwork, worry spread across Jordan's face.

"What?"

Rex bit back his laughter and knocked again. Of course, there was nothing wrong with Omar's face, but considering how nice he'd been to Jordan the past week, he figured the guy was long overdue for a bit of trolling.

A second later, the door opened, and a large Black man poked his head around the corner. "The fuck do you want, Rex? Do you know what time it is?"

"It's noon, my guy. Wake your ass up." Without another word, Rex pushed past him and gestured for Jordan to follow.

"Rex, I should really knock you on your pasty ass for waking me up. Teesha ain't even here. I dropped her off at her mama's house last night."

"I didn't come to see Teesha, actually." He'd been over a few weeks ago to see his goddaughter—an experience that had tripped him out more than he'd expected. It felt like the last time he'd seen her, she was just learning how to walk, but now she was having full conversations with him and asking to play games on his phone.

"Why are you bothering me, then? And who is this?"

"This is Jordan," he said, jerking his head towards the man. "We actually need your help with some shit. I'm paying too, so wake your grouchy ass up and log onto your computer."

Omar and Jordan exchanged a quick raise of chins before Omar gave Rex a dirty look and headed into his office. Like the lawn outside, this room was also decorated with various Barbie dolls and action figures. A small table beside the desk housing a Mac and drawing tablet was littered with cut-up pieces of construction paper, spilled glitter, and an empty box of apple juice. Omar cracked his neck, tapped in his password, and looked back at his guests.

"Y'all can pull up chairs if you want."

Rex grabbed two metal foldout chairs from the closet and set them up for him and Jordan, off to the side of Omar.

"What do you need?" Omar asked. "And how quickly am I getting paid?"

Rex reached into his pocket and slipped two bills across the table. Omar folded them into his wallet, clearly satisfied with however much Rex gave him. All the while, Jordan sat back, watching this play out, with no idea what the hell they were doing here in the first place.

"We need a flyer," Rex said. "Something that'll catch as much attention as possible. It's for a book club."

"Nigga, I know you're not waking me up to work on some bullshit like this," Omar laughed.

"I'm serious," Rex insisted. "It's for a club I'm part of. We're trying to get as many people as we can to sign up for it, and you're the best at that shit. We just need a little flyer. Something that'll get all the old ladies in town excited."

Jordan cleared his throat. "It's, uh—it's a club for reading romance novels."

"You know what? I'm not even about to ask."

Rex shot Jordan a hopeful smile, and a bit of the tension in Jordan's body eased away. After having gone so long without having to defend Meet Cute Club, the potential for conflict had him on high alert.

Thankfully enough, any time Omar made a comment about how silly it all was, Rex shot him down, steering the conversation back to designing the poster. By the end of it, the final product was actually pretty damn incredible. The front of the flyer was designed like the cover of a historical romance, courtesy of a few stock photos Omar put together. The club's name stood out in scrawling lavender letters, and all the relevant information was placed at the bottom of the page.

"Thoughts?" Omar asked, sitting back in his chair.

After a moment of inspection, Jordan smiled. "It's perfect."

"That's what I'm talking about." Omar saved the file, then dropped it into an email to send to Jordan.

Rex slapped his hand down on Omar's shoulder, giving him a squeeze. "You did us a solid today, man."

"Yeah, whatever. You know what you can do? You can take my trash out while you're here, how 'bout that?"

Rex let out a laugh and put his hands up in defeat. "Alright, fine. Least I can do." He turned to Jordan. "Be right back."

Once they were alone, Omar glanced at Jordan once more. "You know I was just fucking with you, right? About the club? We don't really know each other, so I'm not trying to come off like an asshole just yet."

There was something so relieving about Omar coming to him like this. He couldn't be sure whether they were cool enough to talk to each other or not, but surprisingly, even without Rex in the room, he didn't feel awkward at all. Jordan shrugged. "Rex does it all the time. I'm used to it by now."

Amused, Omar said, "You wanna get under his skin and shut his ass up? Tell him his motorcycle's wack. That's a bullet straight through his heart."

"I'll remember that," Jordan said, chuckling softly. "By the way… Did you, uh—did you wanna join the club?"

"Fuck no. But I admire your hustle. Good luck, my man. Hope you guys pull all kinds of new members."

Rex returned a moment later, drying off his dampened hands on his hunter green t-shirt. His eyes darted from Jordan to Omar. "What were you two just talking about?"

Smirking, Jordan rose from his seat and said, "Nothing, nothing. You ready to go?"

"Yup, trash is all taken care of."

"Good looking out," Omar replied.

As the three of them made their way to the front door, Jordan looked back to say, "Hey, thanks again for your help. The flyer looks amazing."

"Keep me in mind if you ever need another one. Leave this dude at home, though. I'd like to avoid him as often as I can." Omar and Rex took a moment to shove each other before Rex led Jordan down to the curb where he'd left his bike. Now alone, Jordan said,

"Thank you for sticking up for me in there. You didn't have to do that."

Rex tossed him the helmet. "I know I didn't. You could've handled yourself. But it's probably tiring as hell doing that all the time. Figured you needed a break."

That statement shouldn't have touched Jordan the way it did. This was a gesture friends made for each other. They stuck up for one another, even when they didn't have to. Still, something about Rex's willingness to speak up, even if Omar was only teasing him, felt like something important.

"Where to now?" Jordan asked. "Never mind. I'll see, right?"

"Exactly," Rex said with a wink.

Their next destination was just as foreign to Jordan, but when Rex pulled into the garage, Jordan knew they were back at his place. Inside, the home looked like it belonged to someone else with all the Precious Moments figurines lining tables and pictures of an older couple hanging from the walls.

"This is your house?" Jordan asked hesitantly.

"For the time being. It was actually my nana's, but since she passed, I'm packing it all up and selling it."

Jordan frowned, his thoughts going to his own grandmother. Would he be strong enough to pack up her place all on his own? He wasn't certain, and he hated even thinking about it in the first place. "I'm sorry for your loss," Jordan said. "What was she like?"

Rex took a seat at the table in the large kitchen, opening his laptop. While he waited for it to load, he looked up at Jordan. Sadness dotted his expression like the freckles on his face, barely visible from afar. "Nana was probably the most amazing woman I ever met—aside from my mom and Amy, of course. The same way the library was a home away from home, this place was, too. She let me spend all summer over here sometimes. Amy wasn't old enough for the first few years, but when she turned five, she would stay with us. That's actually us in that picture up there."

He gestured at one of the photographs hanging on the kitchen wall. As Jordan approached, he got a better look at Rex and his younger sister. Though it was hard to be positive, he was pretty sure that she was the younger woman he'd seen Rex with at Barney's burger shop last month.

They had the same dark chocolate brown hair and thick eyebrows, though Amy's nose was a bit more upturned than Rex's, and she had fuller lips. "You were a cute kid," he commented.

"I'm an even cuter man. At least, that's what I've heard a few times."

"I always wanted a brother or sister," Jordan sighed, taking a seat beside Rex. "My parents said one was enough, so I never got the chance. I think it would've been nice."

"Yeah, Amy's… She's a fucking nightmare most of the time, but I love the kid to death. There aren't many people I'd move mountains for, but that girl? Without question."

There was a resolve in Rex's voice that Jordan

immediately recognized. Whenever he spoke about Sherleen to any of his old coworkers, he could hear it in his own words. To earn that kind of love was a milestone that very few in Jordan's life had ever reached. With how distant his parents had been in his life, Jordan wondered if anyone else but Sherleen had received it.

The sudden whirring of a machine startled Jordan, and he looked across the room to see a printer coming to life. The advanced technology seemed so out of place in the dated kitchen. "Did you buy that for these flyers?" he asked.

"Maybe." The wink that followed was the only answer needed. "I told you, we're gonna save Meet Cute Club because I'm here now. Little did you know, that was all you needed."

Torn between rolling his eyes at Rex's arrogance and pulling the man in for a quick kiss, Jordan decided to fall exactly in the middle, giving him a harmless, "You're so annoying," before crossing the room and grabbing the stack of flyers that had already finished printing.

"These look incredible, Rex," he sighed, pulling them to his chest.

"Omar's the best graphic designer in town. We went to the same school for a couple years back when we were kids. Used to hang out all the time when we were older. Then his corny ass went and had a kid and now all he ever does is take care of his responsibilities. Boring, right?"

"The most boring," Jordan added facetiously.

"I was thinking we can go around town and put the flyers up in different shops and stuff. Maybe somewhere like the Activity Center?" Rex suggested. He rose from his seat and joined Jordan at the printer. Jordan hadn't been lying. They looked great on the computer when Omar was working on them, but in full color, they looked even more spectacular.

"You think this will actually work?" Jordan asked. Rex could see just how anxious he was by the way he held the papers a hair too tight.

He stepped closer, reaching out to take Jordan by the wrist. "Do I have to repeat myself again? Meet Cute Club will live to see another day. I promise."

When Jordan looked up at him with those rich brown eyes, he couldn't help himself. It had been far too long since they'd kissed, and he wasn't letting the perfect moment slip away. He tilted Jordan's head up by the chin, leaned in gradually, and pressed their lips together. Unlike before, he took his time, practicing restraint that he rarely ever had.

Jordan finally stepped back to break the kiss. "I hope you're right," he whispered.

Eight

Maybe they'd been a little in over their heads.

When that following Wednesday afternoon approached and Rex was free to hang and hand out flyers, Jordan found himself elated, energized with the possibility of new members joining the club. There was a pep in his step that, since Lana left the club, he hadn't felt in quite some time. He was even hopeful enough to overlook the ominous signs like accidentally knocking a can of soda onto a stack of flyers and Rex being thirty minutes late because of a wreck on the highway.

The weight of the day they were up against didn't sink in until they began walking through Main Street taping flyers to poles and entering some of the smaller businesses to talk with the owners.

Jesus Suarez, the owner of The Cantina, desperately wanted to let them leave flyers in his store, but he'd already had to turn down a few other people looking to do things in the past, and it wouldn't be fair to make exceptions.

And when they tried handing them out to a group of men entering the Activity Center to work out, they'd been laughed at—as well as threatened after Rex balled up a flyer and threw it at the back of one of their heads. The only thing preventing them from an altercation was Jordan dragging Rex away by the collar.

He tried to keep his spirits high, but victories were far and few between. Jeanie Brown at the You Had to be Hair beauty salon allowed them to leave a few flyers inside, and the nannies taking their kids for walks graciously accepted a few, but those instances only seemed to be hopeful needles in disheartening haystacks.

When they stopped for a quick hotdog from a street vendor, Rex looked at Jordan like a puppy caught digging through a garbage bag. "Look," he started.

"It's not your fault," Jordan said, sighing heavily. "Today's probably just not a good day. We maybe should've tried Saturday or something. People might be in a better mood then."

"I'm willing to go out as many days as we need."

"Maybe we could try a newsletter, too? I've heard those

help," Jordan suggested.

"That might work. Might not get the younger crowd who don't even read their emails, but it could work."

Jordan collapsed onto one of the wooden benches nearby and tried not to let his mood sour too much. None of this was either of their faults, but he couldn't help the bitterness. Rex had gotten his hopes up with how confidently he spoke. He was willing to wager that if the man cleaned up his look a little bit, he could be quite the convincing politician.

Rex took a seat beside him, popped the last of his hotdog into his mouth, and said, "Hey, it's not over until we say it's over. And it's not over yet, got it? I don't care if I have to pose naked in a calendar or something. We'll get more butts in seats."

Jordan eyed the man, halfway considering his idea. "Maybe that's not the worst idea you've had…"

"You just want to see me naked."

"Something tells me you wouldn't mind it one bit. Anyway, you're right. It's not over."

The rumble of thunder overhead startled Jordan, nearly causing him to drop his food. His heart sank as he brought out his phone to check the weather. Despite the forecast telling him there was a light chance of rain, when he turned his head upward to the sky, he could see gray clouds rolling in.

"Maybe it is over," Rex snorted, shaking his head.

"We should go before we get rained on. I knew we should've taken my car instead of walking. So much for enjoying the beautiful day." Jordan made quick work of the rest of his hotdog before he and Rex hustled down Main Street the way they came. It didn't matter how quickly they moved, however, because halfway back, the shower began.

Thunder boomed louder than before, and the frigid rain left Jordan chattering his teeth. The stack of flyers in their hands did little to shield them from the torrent of precipitation. Jordan sped up ahead, leading the way back to his house. Thinking quick on his feet, he took a shortcut. The less time they spent in the drenching rain, the better.

Jordan slammed the front door shut behind Rex, hugging himself to keep warm.

"Holy shit," Rex said. He examined the glob of papers in his hands. There was no hope for them. "Sweet Rose, you're one cruel piece of work. Hey, you okay?" Jordan stood with his arms around his chest, silent as a mouse. "It's not that big of a deal, Jordan."

"It's not," he murmured. "We'll take a rain check on handing out flyers."

Rex cringed at the terrible pun, but that only made Jordan laugh harder. With the day they'd had, laughing released all the built-up tension in his body. He finally unclenched his jaw and relaxed his shoulders, simply letting go and laughing until he felt like he just might be losing it.

"You have issues," Rex said, failing to keep from cracking a smile.

"I need tissues to dry off. Get it? Issues and tissues?" He fell into another fit of laughter, and this time, Rex was unable to hold back as well. He took the stack of papers from Jordan, added it to his own, and tossed them in the garbage.

Jordan watched him, stifling the last bits of laughter fluttering in his stomach. He immediately went quiet as Rex began pulling his jacket from his shoulders, exposing the sleeve of tattoos covering his right arm. A faint dew of water glistened on his biceps, and Jordan practically swallowed his tongue as his eyes roamed the man's body.

Rex then pulled his shirt over his head.

"W-what are you doing?" Jordan asked, his throat drier than anything either of them currently had on.

"You mind if I take a shower? Smelling like wet dog isn't my thing, funny enough."

"Oh. Yeah. You can use the shower upstairs if you'd like. I'll…I'll see if I have anything you can wear."

Making his escape, Jordan bounded up the stairs and rifled through his closet, settling on a pair of gray sweats and an oversized t-shirt he knew would both fit. Jordan even found a spare cloth the man could use as a washrag. He turned around to find Rex standing in the doorframe, clad in only a pair of red boxer briefs that left little to the imagination. Weak to his desire, Jordan's eyes followed the line leading down the side of Rex's thigh.

"Is this the bathroom?" Rex asked, gesturing to the door beside his bed.

"Yeah. Here. These are for you." Their hands brushed as Jordan gave him the clothes, and before he could get away, Rex caught his wrist.

"You should probably get cleaned up, too. Don't want you catching a cold."

"That's the only bathroom with a shower."

Rex's expression didn't change. "Like I said." He headed to the bathroom and left the door open just a crack. A moment later, Jordan heard the shower start.

What the hell was he supposed to do now? Just sit here and wait for Rex to finish? Or did Rex mean what he thought he meant?

This was out of Jordan's comfort zone, and a big part of him just wanted to sit downstairs until it was all over. He wasn't built for this kind of thing. Sure, maybe he did read at least three books a week where this exact situation would lead to a romp in bed, and sure, maybe he did hold those books close and fantasize about what it would be like in real life.

But this wasn't a damn book, and he knew that if he did this, there'd probably be no going back. That fear kept him frozen in place, shivering in his soaked clothes as the sound of Rex humming called out to him.

This could very easily destroy everything they had. It had been long—far too long—since he'd done anything like this. What if romance was a skill he'd stopped using, and now he could never pick it back up? What if he was so terrible at it that Rex cut it short and asked to finish his shower alone?

He couldn't lie to himself.

He wanted this. More than he'd wanted anything in a long time. More than he thought it possible. And here the perfect, shining opportunity was. All he'd have to do was push past that threshold and step into the shower with Rex.

Fuck it.

Fuck it!

Jordan made quick work of his clothes, pulling his t-shirt off and dropping it in the hamper by his closet. His pants followed soon after that, and by the time he got to the door, he wore only a pair of damp plaid boxers. He swallowed hard, counted from ten, and entered the bathroom.

As expected, Rex looked up at him, that cocky half-smirk tugging at his lips. "I was wondering when you were gonna show. Started to get a little lonely in here." Rex reached forward and slid the door to the shower open. Suds of soap raced down his slick chest and around the bush of hair just above his dick.

Refusing to give himself the opportunity to shy away, Jordan stepped out of his own underwear, naked as the day he'd been born, and joined Rex under the hot spray of water. Like their kiss, he was initially uneasy, unsure whether they were actually just washing up or something much more. He was abruptly clued in when Rex pressed behind him, reaching around to grab the green rag hanging from the faucet.

He lathered it up with body wash before dragging it over Jordan's shoulders and down his back. Jordan stood still, his eyes closed as he enjoyed the perfect amount of pressure Rex used on his body. He worked his fingers into Jordan's muscles, both cleaning and massaging him. The motion elicited a moan from Jordan, and Rex chuckled deep and low.

"Turn around for me," Rex murmured in his ear, and following instruction, Jordan carefully spun around. Rex got to work once more, rubbing him down. He stepped close and worked the rag in circles over Jordan's chest, trailing down to his crotch. Without hesitation, he continued his massage, causing Jordan to stir.

Rex stepped even closer, closing the gap between them, and wrapped his hand around Jordan's erection. Another moan spilled from his lips, and he felt himself tense until the man began stroking, twisting his wrist as he reached the sensitive tip. Rex lowered his lips to the thudding pulse in Jordan's neck, where he licked greedily.

Hypersensitive in this area, it practically shattered Jordan the moment he touched him. He groaned deep from his throat, slipping an arm around Rex's lower back. "Yes," he managed to whisper.

Rex's speed increased, pumping Jordan with more haste and constriction. His licks turned to kisses, and when he trailed up to Jordan's mouth, he let his tongue make a reappearance. Dominating the kiss, Rex worked his tongue against the other's, hot and slick as his fist continued to send shivers running through Jordan's entire body.

The younger man whimpered, overwhelmed from the stimulation, and his arm tightened around Rex. He could feel it, the hot sparkle of his oncoming orgasm. It warmed him from the pads of his toes to the hair on his head, and Jordan struggled to remain still, his impulse to chase that feeling until the pleasure finally erupted. It didn't take more than a few seconds for it to hit him.

Rex pumped him hard, wordlessly demanding him to

come for him. Jordan obeyed with little resistance. His head fell back, and his body shuddered, and a moan climbed its way from the deepest part of him, echoing off the walls of the enclosed shower. When he came down from the high, he took Rex's face in both hands, kissing him hard.

He couldn't remember the last time he'd kissed someone like this, both grateful for the satisfaction yet hungry for more, unwilling to let him get away for more than a minute. Rex seemed to have no qualms with his fervor, either. He tugged Jordan closer, chest to chest, and said,

"I want this." His hand slipped from Jordan's upper back to the curve of his ass. "You gonna let me have it, JJ?"

Jordan nodded more eagerly than he might have had he not just been overcome with pleasure only moments before. As it were, he couldn't practice any bit of restraint, peppering Rex's shoulders and neck with kisses.

"Get ready for me," Rex said, finally untangling himself from Jordan. He grabbed a towel from the rack and threw one last look over his shoulder before he returned to the bedroom. Once he was dry, he rolled onto the bed, staring at the ceiling as he waited for Jordan to get prepared. He'd long since learned that it could take some time, but he wasn't in any hurry. Well, most of him wasn't. The incessant throbbing between his legs seemed to have a mind of its own, telling him that if it didn't get some attention soon, there would be consequences. Maybe even dire ones.

Rex didn't have to wait long. Fifteen minutes later, he heard the water cut off, and a few moments after that, the door opened. Jordan somehow looked even better naked, his curly hair damp from the shower and the smell of cedarwood spilling off of him. He stopped at the end table beside the bed and pulled a condom from the tiny box inside. With that and a bottle of lubricant in his hands, he crawled across the bed.

Unable to wait any longer, Rex practically jumped into action, rolling Jordan onto his back, an act that drew out a laugh from him. He parted his legs and crawled between them, folding himself over Jordan to kiss him deeply.

Rex paused their kiss only to bring his fingers to his lips, wetting them carefully before they disappeared between their bodies. A moment later, Jordan felt the pressure against him, gently prodding him open. He took in a slow breath before he allowed himself to relax enough for Rex's fingertips to slide inside.

The feeling stung just a little at first, but Rex seemed aware of it because he offset the pain with more kisses, nipping and tugging at his bottom lip as their mouths worked against one another. Jordan's eyes fluttered closed, and his pulse spiked when Rex inched deeper inside of him.

"Let me in," Rex whispered, his voice sending shivers

down Jordan's spine.

He wordlessly obeyed, back arched and hips rolling to take more.

The two men continued this for perhaps longer than necessary, Rex's fingers plunging into Jordan with varying speeds, curled upwards to stroke the sensitive nerves deep inside of him. Jordan held Rex close, moaning into his mouth as his relentless strokes sent waves of euphoria through him. It was strong enough that when Rex finally pulled free, Jordan's face fell.

"Don't worry," Rex murmured against his lips. "I'm not done with you yet."

Rex sat back on his haunches and reached for the small foil square, tearing it with his teeth. He slipped his condom on easily and applied a generous amount of lubrication around his length, spreading the rest over Jordan. There was something to be said about the way Jordan seemed to settle completely in bed, watching Rex as he lined himself up. Rex had seen the look of terror cross his face at the mere suggestion of bathing together, yet here he was, watching intensely without a hint of unease.

Rex pressed inside of him slow, watching the head of himself disappear beyond the impossibly tight ring of muscle. A wonderful little shudder ran through him, making his knees weak and his stomach flutter, but he persisted, sliding deeper into Jordan.

When Jordan's body finally, graciously gave way and allowed him inside, Rex's toes curled, and a long, deep groan vibrated from his throat. He gave Jordan a moment to become adjusted to him before he drew his hips back. With a quick jerk, he was once again buried to the hilt, caressed by the tight heat of Jordan's body.

His pace was steady, but it quickened with every stroke inside of Jordan. The man beneath him moaned, gripping the backs of his thighs as his back arched in desire. It was beautifully lewd watching Jordan spread himself open, inviting him to fill him over and over again.

Rex held nothing back, planting his hands on the bed on either side of Jordan's head to give himself more leverage. His thrusts were harder, his strokes deeper, and Jordan's entire body burned and vibrated and crackled like lightning.

He turned his head and squeezed his eyes, groaning as his body stretched to accompany every inch of Rex. The sting had only just subsided, substituted for the more powerful ecstasy of Rex's dick. His breathing grew shallower, his lungs barely able to fill before the wind was nearly knocked out of him.

Again and again, Rex sent shockwaves through him and electricity racing down his spine. Jordan could just barely process the string of curses Rex let out. What he could perceive, however, was the man's rough hand on his cheek, cupping his face. He stared up at Rex, saw the man's eyebrows practically threaded together in concentration, and let out a moan that resonated from the deepest part of his chest.

That looked to be the magic word, the crack in Rex's dam, because his hips jerked irregularly and his mouth fell agape, body shuddering as he reached his release. His hips moved violently, with all the finality of punctuation at the end of a sentence.

For a long while, the only sound that filled the room was that of ragged breathing. Rex's heartbeat thudded in his ears, and it felt like a Herculean task just to roll off of Jordan and lie on his back. The peaceful absence of conversation felt like the perfect blanket lying over both of them, weighted with just enough pressure to satisfy them both.

The last time he'd felt this good was nothing more than a distant memory in Rex's mind, slippery each time he tried to recall it. Needless to say, it hadn't compared to sex with Jordan. Despite how chaste and wholesome he acted, Rex had always been certain there was another side to him that would be able to keep up with his own libido. This had just confirmed every last one of his suspicions.

"I was thinking," he said, turning to face Jordan. "You should come help me with this garage sale I have going on next week."

"Mm, that's some sexy pillow talk you have there."

Rex chuckled. "I'm serious."

"Yeah?"

"I'm clearing out a lot of my nana's stuff, and she had boxes full of books that you might like. Figured you might want first dibs before I send the rest to the library for donation." Jordan's eyes lit up, and Rex knew without a doubt that he'd made the right decision in pitching the idea to him.

"That's awfully sweet of you," Jordan said.

"I figured it's only fair since I got rained on trying to help you out with your little club or whatever."

Jordan shoved his shoulder, smiling and rolling his eyes. "Shut up. I'll help you do the garage sale, mostly because I want those books. Maybe we could even pick one and see about reading it for the club."

Rex grimaced hard. "Reading the same porn my grandma did sounds so fun."

"Alright, fine, spoilsport. I'll read them myself then." He was silent, then suddenly added, "I think our grandmas would've gotten along."

Rex turned to face him, propping himself up on an elbow to look down at him. "You think so? Why's that?"

"They both loved the same books. Your nana sounds

really headstrong and kind, just like mine. Plus, mine gets along with basically anyone as long as they don't try to play her."

Rex smiled fondly at the idea of Nana Bailey spending time with Jordan's grandmother for weekly meetings at the book club Jordan told him she used to be in charge of. Nana would've insisted on going, and knowing her, he'd have probably been roped along as well.

Despite how sickly-sweet the idea was, Rex didn't find himself turning away from it. He took in Jordan's toothy smile and the way he seemed to fit perfectly up against his body, and his stomach clenched tight.

"I think they would've been great friends," he said. And he meant it.

Nine

On Saturday morning, Rex was at Jordan's front door before the sun had even risen over the hills. At first, Jordan was confused why the man was waking him up so early, then it hit him. The garage sale. Embarrassed to look so bummy, he invited Rex in and hurried upstairs to get dressed for the day. When he returned, there was more color in his brown skin and not an eye crusty in sight.

"I kind of liked your *Walking Dead* extra look," Rex said as they walked out to the car.

"I'm about to Hershel your ass if you don't shut up," Jordan grunted, climbing into the driver's side of his car.

"Someone's grumpy when they don't get their morning coffee."

"Yeah, no kidding." Jordan hadn't slept well at all the

night before, but he wasn't going to tell Rex that. By this point, he was well-versed in Rex-isms and knew that showing any kind of vulnerability opened him up to potential teasing. The last thing he was going to do was add fuel to the fire or paint a target on his head. That was why, rather than going into detail about his night spent tossing and turning, he headed directly to his favorite gas station.

"Fast Fill," Rex said simply, looking up at the orange and cream-colored logo on the front of the building.

"You ever been here?"

"Nope. I'm a QuikTrip kinda man, myself."

Jordan gave a conceding nod. "Fair enough, that's better than Kum & Go, at least. Fast Fill is *the* convenience store." He hopped out from the car once they were parked and pushed through the glass double doors.

"Jordan!"

He turned to the sound of the familiar voice and was greeted with a shock of pinky-peach hair on Valentin's head. It made his skin look even more tan and was a stark contrast to the thick brown mustache above his lip. "Your hair!" he exclaimed.

"Lana convinced me to do it," Valentin laughed, self-consciously running a hand through it.

"That girl will never not be a terror on all of Sweet Rose."

Jordan had been friends with Valentin back in high school, before Jordan's parents had passed away and he'd had to grow up within the span of a few months. Valentin had been the kind of guy that livened any room, never once shying away from the spotlight and all the pitfalls that came with it. He'd even been the reason Jordan decided to come out to his family—to mixed responses. Still, knowing that he wasn't the only one in school had made him feel comfortable with himself.

Though they'd grown and gone their separate ways, Valentin was still a buddy and never hesitated to give him free coffee and snacks when he showed up. Jordan considered all the other gas stations passable, but none of them held a candle to Fast Fill for this reason alone.

Carrying their breakfast out to the car, Jordan waved at Turner, the other co-owner of Fast Fill as he headed into the building. As unassuming as Turner looked, with his perfectly styled mop of hair, clear golden skin, and well put-together polo and khakis, Jordan had heard of his reputation in school and knew all the trouble he'd gotten into. At the time, it was far too adventurous for him, but he'd always found his tenacity admirable.

"I always forget all the characters here," Rex noted on the way to his home. He unwrapped his breakfast burrito and added, "Sometimes it makes me want to stay here."

Jordan glanced his way. "Are you planning on leaving?"

"Once I get the house sold, yeah. Aside from seeing Amy, there's no point in staying. Too many bad memories."

The tone of Rex's voice told him that the conversation wasn't going to go any deeper than this. Rather than pressing his luck, he smirked and said, "Can't wait for you to sell the house, then." Rex snorted, his mouth almost too full of food to smile back.

After finishing breakfast at Rex's place, the two braced themselves for the long day of work ahead. Jordan's incessant need to make everything perfect and presentable was an unintended perk that Rex quickly came to appreciate. Had he been left on his own, the garage and driveway would've looked like an F9 rolled through town and left Nana Bailey's home a post-apocalyptic wasteland.

Not only that, but as meek as he might've appeared, Jordan had no problem helping him pick furniture up and set it outside as well. Before eight o'clock, they'd moved the dining room set to the garage, as well as her two guest bedroom sets and three racks of her clothes.

"I have to ask," Jordan panted, doubling over after he'd placed down a heavy box of trinkets. "How much shit did Nana have?"

"A lot. She was a high-functioning hoarder. At least, that's what she said. Having cleaned it all up, I'd say she was being generous with the 'high-functioning' part. You don't even want to see half of the crap I threw away."

"And you're done packing everything up?"

Rex scoffed and wiped a bead of sweat from his forehead. Even worn out, Jordan couldn't help but think about how good he looked, all sweaty and squinting from the bright sunlight. "I haven't even touched the attic yet. That's mostly family shit, though. Nothing anyone in town aside from nosy neighbors would want to buy."

"You'd make plenty of money," Jordan noted. In Sweet Rose, a guy couldn't brush his teeth without someone down the street finding out and spreading it to five other people. That closeness was both a perk and a pitfall.

"Nana would come back from the dead to kill me," he chuckled. Rex grabbed a box in the grass and carried it to the fold-out table in the garage. "These are the books, by the way. Finally found the right box."

Jordan's eyes grew to the size of saucers, and he nearly knocked over a rack of clothes to rifle through the box of dusty books. "Holy shit," he gasped, pulling a novel out and inspecting it closely. "This is the only book Vivienne Hallaway ever published."

"Who?"

Jordan made a face like Rex had just asked him the most offensive question ever. "Um…what do you mean, 'who?'

You don't know about our state representative's foray into romance? Back in the '80s, Joan Holmes published a shifter romance that she tried to scrub from existence when she ran for office in the '90s. She basically had it pulled from print, and it was damn near impossible to find. Everyone clowned her for it, but she still won, and the romance community has kind of made a legend out of her."

"So, they're everywhere, then?"

Jordan looked up from the cover of the book he stroked with his finger. "They?"

"Romance writers. It's not just women sitting at home writing while their kids take a nap, yeah?"

"Exactly," Jordan said. "People think of this lonely cat lady substituting affection in real life for fake people kissing, but there are so many people of any gender writing this stuff."

Rex took the book from him and flipped through it. "So many different people reading it, too. Is this thing worth any money?"

"Hell yeah. Goes for a few hundred online, especially one that looks this good."

"Well, it's yours. If you want it."

"Are you serious?" Jordan couldn't believe it. Three years ago, he'd considered splurging and buying a copy off eBay to add to his collection, but he just couldn't justify it.

It was still early on in his obsession with the genre, but he'd always dreamed of one day having a copy of *Claws of Attraction* for his shelf.

Rex shrugged. "Sure. I can't think of anyone else Nana would rather give it to."

Jordan covered his joy by opening the book and flipping through it. This was really his. He almost felt selfish for taking anything else from Nana Bailey's collection, but Rex encouraged it, telling him that she'd want to share. With a little more encouragement, Jordan sifted through the box until he got his fill.

That alone made all the hard work of setting up—and the subsequent time that went into running the sale—worth every last bit of effort.

The garage sale had been far more profitable than Rex had ever imagined possible. They hadn't gotten rid of all of Nana Bailey's belongings like the racks of her clothes or all of her figurines, but what they did sell was quite substantial.

Two of her loveseats had been purchased by one of the managers at the Sunset Village motel, her dishes were now in the hands of a single mother with a huge fetish for posting old china on Instagram, and most surprisingly, nearly all the books Jordan left behind sold quite well.

To treat themselves for a day of hard work and as a sign

of gratitude, Rex offered to buy dinner. Jordan put up no arguments, giving him free rein to choose what they ate.

Vietnamese it was.

Jordan clung to Rex as they drove back to Nana Bailey's home, the bag of food resting in the crook of his arm as he hugged himself tight to Rex's defined back.

With nothing to sit on in the living room, Jordan and Rex settled on the rug near the fireplace. Rex knew it wasn't much, but it was preferable to sitting on wood. He smirked to himself, pleased with possible innuendos and wondering if Jordan might have a different opinion on that.

"Hey, I, uh... I know I probably don't say it often, but thank you," Jordan murmured.

"What are you thanking me for? You're the one who helped me today."

"You gave me all these new books. And you're helping me with Meet Cute Club."

"You ever hear of that saying about scratching each other's backs?" Rex asked. He dug into their bags and handed Jordan his food.

"I know, but I mean it. Thank you. For helping me."

Rex glanced Jordan's way and shook his head. "You and these damn books, I swear. You'll be the first man to ever marry someone's entire bibliography, watch."

"It's just that...this club is all I have right now." Jordan dropped his gaze to the tray of fried rice in front of him, picking at a piece of chicken absently.

"What do you mean?"

Jordan seemed to struggle with his words, but finally he got it out. "Do you remember the day Lana said she'd be leaving the club?"

"Yeah."

"Well, right before the meeting started, I got into it with my boss. They kept asking me to do stuff that wasn't in my job description, and I told them that I refused to do it without a raise."

Rex nodded, covering his full mouth as he said, "Seems reasonable."

"That's what I thought," Jordan snorted. "But apparently, that was just too much for them. They said they wouldn't pay me, and I told them I wouldn't do the work then. Then I basically quit my job. God, I'm so stupid…"

Jordan buried his head in his hands and let out a self-deprecating laugh that Rex felt was too close to a sob. He put down his spring roll and scooted closer to the man.

"You didn't quit your job, Jordan. Those assholes made it impossible for you to work with all the stuff they were throwing at you. You made the right decision."

Jordan shook his head. "It doesn't feel like it."

"I learned a long time ago that these corporations don't

JACK HARBON

give a damn about any of us. Nana died, and my boss wouldn't even give me time off to drive here for her funeral. I quit that very same day."

Jordan looked up at Rex, horror on his face. "They wouldn't let you have a few days off to bury her?"

"Nope. And I don't feel bad about it for one minute. So don't you feel bad about it, either. You'll find a new job, even if you have to work at Barney's or something."

Jordan cracked a smile. "Barney is pretty cool. I bet he'd let me work there in a heartbeat."

"You'd look cute in one of those little blue and white striped uniforms, too."

"Whatever," Jordan chuckled, turning his head to keep Rex from seeing his smile. "Anyway, I just wanted to say thank you for helping me. I lost Lana and my job in the same day. I don't want to lose the club, either."

"I get it, JJ. But that's not gonna happen, alright? You said you got a few people calling about possible membership, right?"

"Yeah, three or four. No definitive answers yet, though."

"Those will come soon enough. Don't worry."

Jordan tilted his head at Rex and asked, "How are you so sure about everything? You talk about things like you already know the outcome."

Rex waited until after he'd mixed chili sauce into his

134

container of pho before he said a word. "I know my own limitations. I know what I'm good at, what I'm capable of, and what's a realistic expectation of myself. I never commit to something I don't think I can do. That way, when I say I can handle something, it always happens."

Rex's tone, though even, seemed jaded, like this knowledge was the silver lining of an entire sea of failures and swings and misses. He'd had to learn this lesson the hard way, witness to a man that knew his own limitations but refused to respect them. A man that left one failed family to try again with another, an act that bore identical results.

Rex drowned his bitterness in the slightly floral flavor of his pho broth.

Jordan picked at his plate of rice. "Sometimes I wish I had that skill. I worry about everything, all the time, forever."

"I know you do," Rex said. "That's why you should listen to me more when I say that things will work out. Just like I can recognize my own abilities, I can see it in other people, too."

Jordan turned to face him, sitting up and crossing his legs. "What do you see when you look at me?"

"I see a nerd with too much time on his hands," he said in a noncommittal tone.

"Seriously, Rex."

Rex sighed and sat up as well. He took a moment to look at Jordan, to *really* study him, before he said, "I see a lot of potential."

Jordan kept his lips pressed tight together.

"I see someone that can do a lot. Anything, really. But he's so high-strung that he always finds himself doubting his ability. Kind of obnoxious in an endearing way, but at the end of the day, if he stopped standing in his own path, he'd be able to move mountains."

Rex felt the knee-jerk reaction to cap his analysis off with a joke, but the way Jordan stared at him, eyes soft and brows forming slopes, he fought back against his natural instinct.

"Rex, that's…"

"It's nothing."

"It's not nothing. Thank you."

Rex's eyes darted between his food and Jordan, and he gave a lazy shrug with one shoulder. "Don't let it go to your head. You're still a nerd."

"And you're a good guy."

Those words shouldn't have been an ice water bath over Rex's nerves, yet there he was, swallowing a lump of food down his bone-dry throat like he was eating gravel and glass. His fleeting gaze found Jordan once again, and, not trusting himself to speak without sounding hoarse, he gave him a short, quick nod.

This was the kind of stuff that made Rex's skin itch like a bad case of the hives. He was allergic to any real affection, and no matter how much sarcasm or snark he gave, none of it protected him from this adverse reaction. He avoided these conversations on purpose, fully aware that despite all his attempts at putting up a barbed wire fence around himself, all it would take was a single moment of intimacy to send a butterfly soaring through the chain links to rest in the pit of his stomach.

"Do you want another spring roll?" he asked, changing the subject entirely.

Jordan didn't fight him on it, either. "Sure," he said, reaching for another. Rex watched him bite down on it after dipping it in peanut sauce.

He wasn't entirely certain, but Rex was convinced Jordan gave him a knowing smile as he ate.

Ten

Jordan was quite impressed with himself. When he'd tried to indulge in his thespian side in high school, he'd been laughed at and told he didn't have the acting chops, yet here he was, smiling at his fellow members of the Meet Cute Club and acting like Rex hadn't just rearranged his insides.

Never in his life had he considered himself a quickie kind of guy, but with Rex, he found himself doing things he hadn't ever thought to do. Things like being bent over the counter and getting a fast one in before any of their guests were expected to arrive.

Jordan began the club meeting as laid-back as he could, but it was hard to keep his eyes from darting to Rex, who seemed all too pleased to have captured his attention this easily. Almost pointedly, Jordan avoided that side of the living room, instead mainly looking at Charles and Gloria. They listened attentively, none the wiser about how hard he was trying to keep from just staring at Rex.

Gloria took up most of the conversation during this meeting, seeing as she had actual experience in the medical field like the heroine of their latest romantic thriller, and Jordan was more than happy to let her speak. These were the moments he got most excited about. Getting to see his friends connect with the characters was always a joy for him.

As he listened, he couldn't help but feel Madeline's eyes on him the entire time. They weren't angry or anything, but he did shift in his seat frequently, trying to block them out. After a few moments of suspiciously staring at Jordan— which he tried his best to ignore—Madeline waited for the room to fill up with other conversations before she lowered her voice and said,

"Is something going on between you and Rex?"

Jordan blinked, stunned by her accurate observation. "N-no… Why do you ask?"

How had she been able to suss that out? Rex came over earlier than usual to help set up, and they were always careful about not getting caught. Aside from the time they'd been interrupted by Charles, he and Rex had mastered the art of playing it cool around the rest of Meet Cute Club.

That was the way it had to be, too. The last thing he

wanted was gossip about him and Rex, especially if things ever went sour. Those situations always ruined the dynamics of friend groups, with everyone taking a side and choosing who they were closer with. The club was already struggling, and a divide like that would only cause more shockwaves to their already crumbling foundation. It was better to not cause any further problems and keep this all to themselves.

"Don't play coy with me," Madeline said with a wry smile on her ruby red lips. "I know what mutual pining looks like when I see it."

"I don't know what you're talking about?"

"Oh, you don't?" She tilted her head and smiled patronizingly at him. "You think we don't notice how Rex is always here before anyone else? How you two are always spending time together, setting up flyers, all of that? Get real, Jordan. We're old, but we're not senile."

Flushing from his neck to his cheeks, Jordan looked away, suddenly overcome with humiliation. They'd tried so hard to keep it just between them, but leave it up to the group of people that could find chemistry in two characters glancing at each other across the room to figure out about him and Rex.

"You can't tell anyone," he said in a low voice. "I'm afraid it'll be weird. And we're not even official or anything."

"No? Huh." She looked over at Rex as he and Charles talked quietly, then glanced back at Jordan. "Huh."

"Huh? What do you mean, 'huh'?"

"Nothing!" She held up her hands to show she was innocent, but that wasn't good enough for Jordan.

"What, do you think there's something more there? He's never said anything to me about it." For all Jordan knew, they were just friends. Friends that hooked up—frequently—and sometimes went on nice, quiet dates together, but friends nonetheless. There'd been no official titles, no moment where they sealed the deal and became exclusive. They were friends with benefits. *Really* great benefits, if he were being honest.

"Look, I don't know much about Rex, but I've been around my fair share of men in my life. And I mean that. Me and men are *no* strangers, okay?" Her raised eyebrows added all the emphasis, and Jordan cracked a smile. There was no doubt about Madeline's foxiness. "I know the look he gives you. It's not just a quick glance. He holds on you longer than anyone else. He watches the way your mouth forms words. He's probably told you it means nothing, but…"

As Madeline trailed off, Jordan found himself turning to Rex again. Though he was in the middle of a conversation with Charles, he held Jordan's gaze longer than he might've for anyone else, and the corner of his mouth tugged up just a millimeter.

"Oh," Jordan said, turning back to Madeline. She sat back on the couch, smirking confidently.

"See? I'm never wrong. I've been around the block and read enough of these books to know when there's something there, and Jordan? There's something there. He knows it like I know it. You better go get your man."

Jordan chewed on his bottom lip and sent another fleeting glimpse Rex's way, his entire face growing hotter by the second. Did he really have feelings for Jordan that weren't as casual as he made the situation out to be? Or was Madeline projecting, trying to translate romantic gestures from books into the real world?

He watched Rex for a second longer, his curious thoughts too hard to ignore. It was such a contrast, seeing the way Rex had first entered the club compared to where he was now. Rather than sitting silently, he'd actually begun participating in the conversation more, even mentioning novels he was looking forward to reading later that month.

In a way, Jordan was proud of him. Sure, he had his troll tendencies still, but the level of seriousness he brought to Meet Cute Club was something that only seemed to invigorate the rest of the group. Charles, for example, could hold a thirty-minute conversation with Rex like it was nothing, when Jordan had often struggled to include him in every topic. Smiling to himself, Jordan turned back to Madeline, and embarrassingly enough, she gave him a matching, knowing smile.

Despite being knee-deep in a conversation about the latest paranormal romance he'd read, when Rex's phone vibrated and he saw Amy's number, he excused himself from the conversation and stepped away. In the kitchen, he finally had the privacy to talk.

"Hey, kid," he said in a low tone. "Everything okay?"

Whenever Amy called, that rarely meant anything good. Like most of the younger crowd, she avoided calls at all costs, instead opting to send him texts. In her words, calling was "too formal."

The last time she'd called him, it had been to tell him about Nana Bailey's passing a few months ago.

"Hey," she said, though she could barely be heard over the sound of crying babies and chatty toddlers in the background. "Mom just stopped by to see me at work. She was a complete nervous wreck."

Rex raised an eyebrow and crossed his arms. "What for?" He could so easily picture Georgia bursting through the doors of Little Moments, hair pointing this way and that, startling all of the children under Amy and her coworkers' care.

"It's about Dad," Amy murmured. "She talked to him for the first time since he said he was leaving her."

"Oh. What...what'd he want?"

"Well, he wanted some of his stuff back from the house more than anything else."

"Asshole," Rex muttered. If he were alone, he wouldn't have bit his tongue as hard as he did. He wouldn't mince words or keep his true emotions buried beneath the surface. He was in Jordan's home, though, and he didn't need anyone seeing him get that way, no matter how easy it was for Alan to take him there.

Amy laughed bitterly. "That might be too generous of a compliment. Anyway, Mom said they talked for a while, and that he agreed to go to dinner with her."

Now Rex was really fucking confused. "Wait, why? Please don't tell me she's going back to him, Amy."

With the way Georgia had come into his life, by way of playing a part in ruining his own mother's marriage, he had very little to give the other woman besides the shallow acknowledgement that they were both inextricably tied to the same selfish person. Still, the idea of her running back to the man that cheated on her made him feel oddly disappointed, like he'd expected better of the woman who'd gotten Alan the same way she was now losing him.

"No," Amy said, and Rex sighed with relief. Her mother

was a lot of things, but he was glad astoundingly gullible wasn't one of them. "Mom said she wanted to get dinner with him for closure. A way to say goodbye for good."

"Did she not already say it when she followed him and his new girlfriend to that hotel? Sorry, that was cruel."

"It's fine," Amy said. Rex wasn't so sure he believed her, and kicked himself for not being more considerate of Amy.

"Did Dad say he was going?"

"Actually...he did. She told me that and I almost didn't believe her. I mean, that sounds nothing like him."

"He left my mom without a second thought. Dinner with the second ex-wife is weird," Rex said.

"Maybe he's turning over a new leaf." There was a long pause before the two of them snorted with resentment.

"Yeah, right," Rex said with a sigh. "I don't think this is smart, Amy."

Rex knew a bad idea when he heard one, like 5-in-1 shower gels and reality TV stars turned presidents. Georgia sitting down with Alan and trying to get closure was a disaster waiting to happen. As the eldest of Alan's two children, he'd spent his entire life waiting for that closure. She wasn't going to get it over endless soup and breadsticks.

"You don't?"

"Not really, no." It killed him to crush her hopes like this, but Amy needed to know the truth. She hadn't been around to see the damaged state Alan left his mother in. She might've gotten a glimpse in her own mother's failed marriage, but the first fallout had been the worst.

"I don't know if I should go, then."

"She wanted you to be there too?"

"Yeah," Amy said. "She asked if I'd come for emotional support. I told her I would go no matter what."

Rex held back another sigh. Of course, she agreed to go. Amy was as bleeding as hearts could come, always willing to throw herself on the grenade to protect those around her. There was no way in hell she'd turn her mother down, especially not in a moment like this.

"You should go," Rex said.

There was a moment of silence on her end before he heard the hopefulness in her voice as she asked, "Would you come with me? As *my* emotional support?"

"Fuck, Amy," he groaned. He wanted to say no. God, he wanted to turn her down and tell her that the less he saw his father, the better. But forcing his lips to form the single-syllable word was like pressing similar ends of magnets together. He choked on it, his throat squeezing tight to fight back against his immediate response.

"Please, Rex? It's just one night, and then Mom is gonna leave Dad alone and move on."

"Fine. I'll go."

Rex would've rather licked the soles of everyone in Meet Cute Club's shoes than spend more than a passing moment with Alan, but there he was, begrudgingly agreeing to split a 2-for-20 with the man who'd destroyed more happy homes than every termite combined. He fought to keep the sour tone out of his voice, but it was like running through quicksand, the weight of the situation pressing him deeper into the dark.

"Thank you, Rhett. I love you."

The quick pang in his chest was a reminder that this was all for her. He'd squeeze diamonds from coal if it meant making Amy happy. Being around his shitty sperm donor for an hour or two would be tolerable, much in the same way as a quadruple wisdom tooth extraction with no general anesthesia was.

"I love you too, kid. And remember, you owe me."

"I owe you," she said. He could hear the smile on her face as she spoke. "I have to get back to work, but I'll text you the details later. Love you, bye!" A moment later, the call was over. He slipped his phone into his pocket and shook his head. Sometimes he wished he could go back to not caring about anything but himself. There were a lot fewer uncomfortable social events to attend that way.

When he turned to head back to the living room, Jordan stood a few feet away, watching. Realizing he'd been caught snooping, Jordan diverted his eyes and scratched at the back of his head.

"Hey, nosy," Rex said.

"You okay? You looked upset earlier. Just wanted to check on you."

Rex could only smile at the fact that he had taken notice of his absence, or even watched long enough to read his body language. "I'm fine. Just family stuff."

"Wanna talk about it?"

The only person to ask him something like that in the past few months was Amy. Rex would've been touched by the offer if he wasn't so annoyed with the outcome of his conversation.

"Typical shit," he said with a shrug. "My dad. I'd rather not be around him. My sister roped me into it. So, the worst family dinner possible will be happening soon."

All of Rex's demeanor seemed to show that he didn't care, from his shrugging to the lack of interest in his voice, but Jordan had spent long enough around him to pick up on his tells. He buried his hands in his pockets when he wanted to look above it all, his gaze shifted somewhere else rather than looking Jordan head on, and his sentences grew shorter and more direct.

"You could always say you got food poisoning and skip it," Jordan offered.

"My sister would kill me. I'm only going because of her. 'Emotional support' or whatever it is that she called it."

Jordan stepped closer to him, reaching out to brush his fingers with Rex's. "I could always go with you, if you wanted? Y'know, for emotional support." Jordan said it as a joke, but there was an undercurrent of seriousness in his words. He didn't mind being there if Rex needed him.

"You'd hate it. I don't want you meeting my old man anyway. He's a dick."

"I love dick," Jordan grinned, and to his pleasure, the vulgar joke put a smile on Rex's face too. "I'm serious. I can go with you if it makes the whole thing easier on you."

"Why?"

Jordan made a face. "Why not? You've done so much to help me. I want to return the favor. Plus, I wanna see you take off your motorcycle jacket and put on one for something fancier." He stepped closer again, nearly chest-to-chest with the man. "It'll be more fun with me there, I bet."

"Maybe," Rex said, looking away.

"You know I'm right. Just say yes."

Rex took a moment to think before he looked down into Jordan's rich brown eyes. "Fine. But only if you wear something nice, too."

"Like a suit?"

"The only suit I want to see you in is your birthday suit."

"Twice in one day?" Jordan asked, pecking Rex on the lips. "Help me finish the meeting first and maybe you'll get to see me in it again."

Rex rested his hands on Jordan's hips and kissed him softly. "Deal."

Eleven

What was the perfect outfit to wear when meeting someone you were sure you weren't going to like? Jordan knew that he wanted to dress up, considering they'd be heading to a fancy French restaurant a few miles from his house, but he couldn't decide what image he wanted to present when he finally met Alan Bailey.

"You're stressing over nothing, boy," Sherleen said, her voice sounding tinny over the speaker of Jordan's phone. "Just toss something on and get your ass out there."

"It's not nothing, Grandma," he whined. "It's a big deal. At least…I think it is." This wasn't the conventional Meet the Parents moment he'd anticipated. Hell, if Rex had it his way, Jordan was pretty certain he wouldn't meet Alan at all.

Part of him wanted to know more about the mess, but a

larger, more supportive part told him that it didn't matter. No matter how Alan was tonight, he was there to support Rex and make this whole thing just a bit more tolerable.

"Wear a button-up and some slacks, since you wanna dress all uppity for this man," Sherleen mumbled. "Something white. You look good in white."

Jordan blushed and reached for his favorite white dress shirt, pulling it from the hanger. He slipped into it and buttoned it all the way to the top. With a dark gray tie and his well-tailored slacks that made his butt look nice, he felt pretty damn presentable with minimal effort. This was his style, anyway. Casually dressy.

"Hey, when are you coming to see me again? I just got another recipe from Powell that I want to try out."

Jordan rolled his eyes and flopped on his bed. "I'm not sure. Besides, you can't keep letting this man give you his whole cookbook."

"And why the hell not, boy?"

"You're gonna fatten me up if you keep forcing all these treats on me!"

"Yeah, well, you could do to put a little more weight on. You're too skinny."

"Rex likes it," Jordan muttered without thinking. His eyes went wide a second before Sherleen got onto his case.

"Jordan, don't make me come over there and whoop

your ass. Don't be getting all nasty on my phone."

Stifling his laughter, he said, "I'm sorry, Grandma, I'm sorry!" His phone vibrated on the nightstand, and when he grabbed it, he found a text letting him know that Rex was outside. "Hey, I gotta go, he's here."

"Alright, baby, you have fun. Call me back later. And bring your black ass over here to see me!"

"I will, I will! Love you!"

The moment the call was over, he hopped up from the bed, paused to check himself out in the mirror, and grabbed his keys from the desk in the corner of the room. He looked fine. This would be fine. It would all be fine.

"Let's take your car," Rex said when Jordan locked his front door behind him. "Don't wanna get any dirt on you." Rex reached for Jordan's hand, raised it, and spun him around. "You clean up nice, JJ."

The warmth of his compliment spread through Jordan like a ripple. "Whatever," he grumbled, though he was certain that both of them knew how affected he'd been by the kind words. "You look good too, I guess."

In the car, Rex turned to Jordan and said, "You ready for the worst dinner of your life? I think Robb and Catelyn Stark probably would've preferred their dinner to this one."

"I didn't watch your dragon show, Rex. And don't worry. I've sat through plenty of awkward family dinners, and you don't have a horse in this race. You're here for Amy, I'm here for you. Two hours, that's it." He let go of the steering wheel to give the other man's hand a firm squeeze. "Don't sweat it."

Rex appreciated the gesture, but only he knew the truth. He'd borne witness to just how unconscionable his father could be when he wanted to. He'd seen the trail of flames and destruction left behind while the man walked away unburned. All he could do was cross his fingers and hope that this would all be as easily digestible as his Coq au Vin.

The drive took no time at all, and as they parked, Rex glanced to his left to find his sister, father, and Georgia standing underneath the striped awning. Amy wore a simple black dress and shawl, while Georgia looked like she'd just buried her rich husband who'd died under "mysterious" circumstances. In a red gown that revealed enough cleavage to feed a village of hungry children and suited her auburn hair to perfection, Rex could've easily mistaken her for a Jessica Rabbit stunt double. Toss in a pair of purple gloves, and he was sure her outfit could pass as casual cosplay.

"Finally," Alan grunted as Jordan and Rex approached. "Any reason you're so late?" he asked his son pointedly.

"Traffic?" Rex offered. Unamused, the man shook his head and stormed into the restaurant without another word. Amy gave Rex an exasperated look while Georgia sashayed after her ex-husband.

"Hi," Jordan said, shaking Amy's hand. "I'm Jordan, Rex's—"

"Little boyfriend, I know," she said cheerfully.

"I—"

"Amy, you know he's—"

But before she let either of them get much more than that out, she winked, turned on her heels and headed into the restaurant. Rex's temples throbbed. Not even five minutes with the family, and he could already feel a migraine coming on.

"Sorry about Amy. She's…"

"She's great," Jordan laughed. He laced his fingers through Rex's and gave him a tug. "C'mon, 'little boyfriend.'"

Rex groaned but allowed himself to be dragged inside. At the table, Alan and Georgia sat on opposite ends facing each other while the rest filled in the gaps, Jordan by Rex's side. Wine and drinks came first, and it took all he had not to curl his lip in disgust as Alan made quick work cracking open a bottle of red and nearly filling his glass to the brim.

"So," Georgia said, leaning forward to expose more of her chest. "What've you been up to, Alan? Anything exciting?"

"No."

Rex was unfazed, but the man's curt response seemed to shock Georgia. She blinked quickly, caught off guard, but recovered with ease. "That's too bad. I've been quite busy with work. It's hard to find time to date, but I've found a way to make that work as well."

Rex shot Amy a look, and she shook her head once. A lie.

It all became clear, just like that. As much as she wanted closure, more than anything, Georgia wanted to show him that she wasn't just another disposable woman in his life. A notch in his overpriced imported headboard. She didn't need him. The only issue was that Rex doubted Alan would even give a damn.

"Congratulations," Alan said, tapping away on his phone without looking up. "What's taking the waiters so long?" he asked loud enough to draw attention from the staff. Immediately, a man came hurrying over, vehemently apologizing for not being there sooner.

"Can I start you off with anything? Any appetizers?" the man asked in an accent Rex considered a little *too* put on to be authentically French.

As the rest of them ordered, Jordan flipped through his menu, trying to find something that he could say out loud without embarrassing himself. Mispronouncing an entrée during a Meet Cute Club outing was one thing, but something told him Rex's father wouldn't be all too pleased to hear him butcher the language of love.

"I'll have the beef bourguignon," he said simply, handing over his menu.

"Fantastic! I'll have that out for you soon."

Alan snorted. "Hopefully faster than it took to get some service."

The server's face flushed as red as the wine in Alan's glass, and he excused himself, hurrying off to the kitchen. Jordan's adrenaline spiked despite the stillness of his body. Apathy was one thing, but being rude to waiters and embarrassing them like that? That was as tacky as the diamond-encrusted watch on Alan's wrist.

The conversation while they ate was light, and Jordan watched as Georgia did her best to put on a brave face. He could see the tiny cracks in her armor; the way her face sank every time she waited for some kind of praise that never came, or how her confident smile fell the moment Alan busied himself with his meal or his phone.

It was like watching a soap opera live, only he couldn't find any kind of pleasure in the melodrama. These were real people, and though he might not have cared about all of them equally, it still felt wrong to be amused by Georgia's desperation, or the way Amy picked at her salad uncomfortably, never once actually taking a bite.

JACK HARBON

Even Rex's snappy wit was temporarily neutered, his tail between his legs as he listened to his father go on and on about work and how well stocks were doing. Jordan could only stare at the scene unfolding with genuine sadness, like every dynamic in the family was broken and Rex was the only one honest enough to talk about it.

"You know," Georgia started, another fake smile on her face, "I'm so glad we got to have this dinner together, actually. I think it's so mature that we can—"

Alan's shrill ringtone cut her sentence short, and he held a finger up, excusing himself from the table without acknowledging that she'd just been talking. Once he was out of earshot, Georgia turned to Amy.

"I'm trying," she said, her voice barely above a whisper. Amy placed a thin hand on top of her mother's and rubbed her knuckles tenderly.

"I know, Mom."

"He's just making it so hard."

"You should've known," Rex said under his breath.

"Rex," Amy hissed, shooting him a deadly glare.

Georgia sat back in her chair. "He's right. I should've known that this would happen. I guess... I guess I just thought that maybe he'd show some kind of...anything, really. It's like he's completely cut off his feelings for me, even the bad ones. I thought I could at least get a rise out of him. Some kind of sign that he still cares, even a little bit."

Jordan wanted to offer Georgia some kind of consolation, but rather than reaching out the same way Amy did, he silently picked at his plate, giving her somber eyes that he hoped communicated everything he was feeling.

Alan returned a few moments later, a wide smile on his face. "Sorry about that," he said, looking around at all of them. "Jennifer."

"Who's Jennifer?" Georgia asked.

"Oh, I didn't tell anyone? Jennifer's the woman I've started seeing. Gorgeous, blonde, probably just graduated."

"Hopefully college and not high school," Rex said.

Alan's eyes slid to Rex with unfiltered disdain. "Of course it's college."

"You didn't tell me you were seeing anyone." Georgia's voice was soft, frail and wavering. It was as if all the gusto from her performance before had been drained. She dropped the air of confidence and stared at Alan with genuine hurt dancing on the brim of her eyes.

"I just did," he said, shrugging.

"Jesus," Jordan whispered. He hadn't meant to say anything, especially about something this personal. Sherleen had always taught him to stay out of other people's business, particularly when it came to relationships, but he couldn't help the shock that escaped him listening to how callous Alan was.

"I can't believe you," Georgia said.

"You're the one that was just bragging about all the men you're sleeping with, sweetheart. You can't believe *me?*" Alan looked around, waiting for someone to agree with him. What he found was three sets of downcast eyes and the sound of other customers' conversations. "Now I'm the bad guy?" he laughed incredulously.

"No," Georgia said, wiping tears from her eyes. "I'm just a goddamn idiot." She forcefully pushed herself from the table and took off towards the bathroom, hands covering her face.

"Mom, wait!" Amy stood up and chased after her, leaving only the men sitting around the table in a semi-circle. The weight of silence pushed down on Jordan like a hydraulic press, and he shifted in his seat uncomfortably.

Rex, however, was never one to hold back his thoughts, and he simply stared at his father with a humorless smirk.

"What?" Alan asked irritably.

"You know what."

The older man sighed and shook his head. "One day, you'll get tired of hating the man that gave you everything you have in life. It must be utterly exhausting."

"Not particularly," Rex said with a shrug. "It's pretty

damn easy, honestly. I mean, I can't do it as easily as you can walk away from all of your responsibilities, but I manage."

"Please, I've given you nothing but the best, Rhett."

"I'm not talking about just me. I'm talking about you not being there for Amy. I'm talking about me having to clean up *your* mother's house because you were too busy to do it yourself. I'm talking about you having to be convinced to go to Nana's fucking funeral."

Jordan's stomach clenched hard, and he placed his hand on Rex's knee, a subtle reminder to try to keep calm. While it wasn't his place to tell these two not to do this, he also knew Rex. He knew his temper, and though he'd never seen him get this heated, there was an electricity to it that he recognized.

"I'm not going to sit here and be insulted over a dinner I'm paying for."

"I have a fucking job, Alan. I don't need anything from you."

"What, that pathetic little part-time bookstore gig? What're you going to do when that falls through and you get bored of it? Skip town and wander the country like you did before? You talk about me running from my responsibilities, but what about you? You'll leave like you always do. Homeless by the end of the year. And when you are, don't expect me to bail you out again or give you any money," Alan spat, leaning forward so that he could lower his voice and still get the point across.

"What you seem to forget is that I don't depend on you anymore," Rex said through gritted teeth. "You waving your money around won't work on me anymore. Nobody here needs you to pay for anything. You don't get to throw it back in our faces and use our desperation as a way to get us in line. And when you're all alone with your money, you can buy all the fancy cars and stupid ass watches, but you'll still die by yourself, and frankly, I wouldn't wish spending eternity with you on anyone. Not even you."

Alan smiled back with that same angry grin, and Jordan could see how alike they were. Where he'd gotten it from. Watching them go at it was like Rex fighting with a twisted carnival mirror. As different as they appeared, there were similarities that proved they were undeniably linked together.

"Enjoy your dinner," was all Alan said. He rose from his seat, tossed his napkin on his plate, and strode out of the room without even looking back.

Jordan tried to swallow down a gulp of his wine but it turned his stomach. He'd thought Rex was being hyperbolic, but after having met the man, he really should've taken his verdict far more seriously. "Dick" didn't even begin to cover all that Alan was.

Jordan reached out for Rex, and to his surprise, Rex didn't pull away from him. He turned to face him, offering a hopeful look. "I'm fine. It's fine."

But Jordan knew it wasn't, and judging from the way their conversation had gone, it probably wouldn't ever be fine.

Twelve

Dinner didn't last much longer after Alan's departure. Rex lost his appetite, and when Georgia and Amy returned from the bathroom, Jordan could see that Rex wasn't the only one. Amy, bless her heart, tried to keep the mood up, but the moment Georgia found out that Alan had left without so much as a goodbye, it was obvious that dinner was officially over.

Amy's shoulders sank, and she sat back in her chair, arms folded across her chest. She waited for Georgia to head outside before she said, "I think I might hate him, Rex."

Despite the rage bubbling inside of him, he managed to offer her a sympathetic nod. "I know, Ames. He's the worst."

"Why come here when we could've just eaten the rich,"

Jordan said. Amy and Rex laughed quietly, but still, the sour mood persisted.

"Let's get out of here," Rex said finally, tossing his napkin on his plate of lobster and standing from his seat. Neither of the other two needed to be told twice. After Amy and Rex shared a long hug, Jordan followed Rex back to the car.

The ride back was uncomfortably quiet, but Jordan filled the silence humming along to the radio. Throwing occasional glances in Rex's direction, Jordan could see that he wasn't in a good mood, but he didn't know what to say. He wanted to cheer him up somehow, make him laugh or take his focus off his father, but these kinds of things often ran deeper than a simple joke could repair.

Outside of Nana Bailey's house, Jordan pecked him on the lips and said, "Have a good night, okay?"

Rex nodded without much enthusiasm. "Sure." Jordan started to head back to his car when Rex caught his arm. "Hey," he said. "You, uh...you wanna stay the night?"

From Rex's demeanor, Jordan knew that he probably needed him there more than he would ever actually say, and before he even had a chance to consider it, he said, "Of course." With the night they'd had, he couldn't imagine saying no to Rex. After all the shit Rex had been there for when it came to Jordan's personal life, it was only fair.

Inside, the two of them made quick work of removing their clothes and getting ready for bed. They climbed into the shower together, this time actually managing to clean each other without touching longer than necessary. While Jordan spent some time detangling his hair and moisturizing, Rex slipped on his underwear and headed to the bedroom.

Jordan swiped a small circle in the fog and faintly smiled at his reflection. This was the first night he'd ever spent with Rex, and something about that made his stomach do one of its tiny little flips. Rather than mulling over that feeling, he finished detangling and, to his surprise, found a leave-in conditioner that was close enough to his own at home.

Stepping out of the foggy, humid bathroom and flicking off the light, Jordan found Rex lying flat on his stomach in bed, tapping away at his phone. He wore only a small pair of black boxer briefs, and even though his face was turned away, Jordan still admired how effortlessly handsome he looked.

Quietly, he climbed across the bed and straddled Rex, placing his hands on the man's shoulders. "What are you doing?" Rex asked, looking back at him.

"You look tense." Jordan pressed his thumbs deep, massaging Rex's shoulders with what he hoped was enough pressure. Rex, clearly enjoying the impromptu massage, put his phone down and let his head fall to the mattress.

"That feels good," he said quietly, his voice coming out in a groan.

Jordan smiled. "Good."

As he worked his hands lower down Rex's body, he leaned forward to press kisses to his shoulders and the back of his neck. Rex smelled fresh, like he'd spent time lathering up his body wash to rid himself of their dinner with Alan. Like he'd scrubbed himself clean of all that negativity.

Jordan's palms slid over Rex's shoulder blades smoothly, and he trailed them down his back, feeling every little muscle and knot buried beneath his skin. His kisses continued to follow, this time dotted over every freckle on the man's back. He took his time, enjoying the feeling of Rex below his fingertips. Very rarely did he get this kind of intimacy. Jordan wasn't going to let it go to waste this time.

When he pulled away, Rex made a noise of protest. Jordan smiled. "What?"

"Don't stop," he said quietly.

"You want more?"

"Please."

"Tell me what you want, Rex," Jordan said, burying his face in the crook of Rex's neck and kissing his warm skin once more.

"I want you to distract me," he said. "Make me forget

about tonight. End the night on a high note."

Rex could hardly believe the words he was saying. This wasn't like him, this kind of gnashing, churning desperation inside of him that practically had him clinging to the sheets. There was no dishonesty to his words, though. He wanted to forget it all, to pretend like he hadn't allowed his father to anger him so much. He wanted to wipe Georgia's disappointed face from his mind and pretend like he hadn't witnessed her realize the same things he had years ago.

Jordan obliged without another word, kissing his way down to Rex's lower back. He grabbed at the waistband of Rex's underwear and slid them down past his knees, then his ankles. Now completely bare, Rex found himself being pulled up onto his knees and Jordan spreading him apart.

"Fuck," he breathed, torn between wanting to take control and give it at the same time. The combination terrified him, but when Jordan began stroking him with his tongue in slow, languid motions, physicality beat out rationality, and he allowed himself to ease back into the man's hands, rolling his hips in encouragement.

Jordan lapped at him like nothing else mattered, taking his time as he explored a part of Rex so few had ever gotten the chance to. He relished in the moans the man made, how easily they could go up in pitch the deeper he went. And when he was sure Rex was on the edge of his seat and starved for something a little more satisfying, he prepared himself with a condom and more than enough lubrication to help the whole process move smoothly.

God, Rex had forgotten the sting in the beginning. It had been too long since he'd bottomed for anyone, but the lack of frequency only made him want it more. He braced himself and groaned through the stretch, eyes tight and fists clenched in the sheets. Jordan balanced it with all the works, turning his head so that they could kiss and reaching around to stroke his aching arousal.

The ease of Jordan's movements was the biggest surprise. How could someone who looked so good on his back also be this good in the opposite position? For as good as it felt, Rex was annoyed. Of course, Jordan would be good at everything.

The sudden jerk of Jordan's hips was exactly what he needed to get him out of his head, because the moment he felt their bodies press flush together, he gasped and his mind spun. "Yes," he grunted, thrusting back to meet him. "Harder."

Jordan happily obliged, pulling his hips back and thrusting forward once more, connecting their bodies with more force than before. That seemed to do wonders, judging from the way Rex threw his head back in pleasure. Sensing the other man's preference for the rougher side of things, Jordan wrapped his hand around Rex's bared throat. He added no pressure. The groan that he felt vibrate beneath his fingers was evidence that his hand being there was more than enough.

He buried himself inside of Rex repeatedly, one hand around his throat while he held his waist with the other. When the burn of his speed was too much, Jordan nearly folded himself over the other man and rolled his hips, stirring steadily. Once he could go again, he began thrusting just as hard, filling the room with the sound of bed squeaks, Rex's satisfied groans, and skin slapping against skin.

Rex turned his head and reached back, pulling Jordan down into a needy, desperate kiss that quickly slipped into messy territory, their tongues brushing together like they were battling for control. Unsurprisingly given the reversal of roles, Jordan won, breaking away to trail kisses down his cheek, beard, and throat.

This was all such new territory for Jordan, but he accepted it with open arms, eventually kneeling upright again. He held onto Rex's hips hard and began tugging him back, giving him some encouragement.

"There you go," he moaned. "Show me you want it."

Rex smiled darkly over his shoulder and began pressing backward to meet him, chills running down his spine with every movement. It was almost too much, seeing that devious look in Jordan's otherwise innocent eyes. Rex couldn't realize the last time he'd gotten this lost in sex before, but he swam as deep as he could, groaning when Jordan seized control once more.

"Yes, yes," Jordan huffed out breathlessly. He was right there, and seeing the way Rex bounced against him with that much yearning had him practically seeing stars.

Rex didn't realize how close he was until he felt Jordan gripping his hips and erratically fucking him. There was something undeniably sexy about seeing Mr. High-Strung lose all his concerns and chase after that feeling like it was the last thing he'd do. Just as Jordan's grinding began to settle, Rex felt his own warmth growing from the pit of his stomach.

He gripped himself hard and stroked only four times before he released, his mouth falling open and a steady stream of grunts spilling free. He finished on the thick comforter beneath them, something he'd worry about cleaning up in the morning. For now, his biggest concern was prolonging the pleasure that made his head spin like vertigo and every nerve in his body hypersensitive.

Jordan kissed the back of his neck and his shoulders as Rex came, his breath escaping in pants. Without even seeing the front of him, Jordan was certain Rex had never looked more attractive than this, consumed with euphoria and practically shivering in his pleasure's aftershocks.

When the spike in Jordan's adrenaline finally calmed down, he rolled onto his back and pressed close to Rex, draping an arm over his chest. "That was okay, right?"

"That was perfect."

Jordan smiled with satisfaction, finally able to relax. Anxiety was a friend he couldn't quite shake in any other instance, but it was particularly bad when it was time for him to perform. Knowing he'd given Rex what he needed was a cough drop down a sore throat.

For a long time, the two of them lay together, staring up at the ceiling as the sound of cars passed by the windows. Rex usually found the noise comforting, especially when it followed a nightly orgasm, but tonight it didn't do the trick. Everything was perfect, from the temperature of the room to the way Jordan's body felt pressed against his, but it all felt wrong. Like he was undeserving of it, like he'd cheated to win. It was an intrusive thought he couldn't free himself of.

Even after Jordan eventually fell asleep and filled the room with the soft breaths of his dreams, Rex shifted uncomfortably, unable to force his eyes closed for very long without being haunted by the fight with his father. Their argument had left him rattled, and despite what he'd told Jordan on the way home, things *weren't* fine.

Deep down, he knew that no matter how horrible his father had been in the past, Alan was right about one thing. He was a runner. He always had been, even as a kid listening to his parents greet each other via screaming matches. He ran to the library. He ran to Nana. It didn't matter where he was going, so long as it was away from the mess he'd found himself in.

He'd run away from Sweet Rose, too.

This realization was like a metronome in his mind, never leaving him for more than a beat before returning to center stage. Frustrated with himself, he slipped out from under Jordan's arm without waking him and headed to the bathroom. There, he flicked on the stark light and blinked at the harshness. His reflection looked as exhausted as he felt.

Confirming his father's point yet again, Rex was hit with the same overwhelming urge to turn away. To look at something else so that he didn't have to look himself in the eyes. This time, he refused. Rex gripped the edges of the porcelain sink and met his own gaze hard. He could walk the other direction from a lot of things, but not himself.

In staring at his own face, Rex identified the proverbial gnat flying around his head, buzzing incessantly. It wasn't just that Alan's assessment had been correct. It was that for the first time in his life, he wished he didn't run. Rex couldn't fool himself into thinking he was someone he wasn't. He'd seen too many times before how trying to force things to work only led to heartbreak. He couldn't force himself to stick around. One day, something would send him racing away from Sweet Rose the same way he'd left years before. The difference now was that he'd be leaving Jordan in his wake.

The thought made him feel sick unlike anything else had. He'd been around Jordan enough to know that the man was fragile. He protected himself with biting snark, but the truth was that his barbed wire was there to protect a heart that bruised far too easily. A means to keep himself safe from the heartlessness of any Sweet Rose suitors.

But he'd turned off the electric fence and let Rex in. He'd made the very mistake that caused him to put up the walls in the first place. Rex wouldn't assume the best of himself. He couldn't possibly do that, not given his history. He knew his limitations and knew what was feasible. Being the man that Jordan needed just wasn't in his wheelhouse.

The thought made his eyes water, and he pressed his palms roughly against his face, stopping them. "Goddammit," he hissed, holding his breath to try and contain his emotions. He didn't do this anymore. He'd taught himself to keep it under wraps years ago, but the thought of Jordan being broken up because of him sent prickles of shame down his body and guilt bubbling up from his throat. It wasn't right, and he knew it.

The knock at the door made him jump. "You okay in there?" Jordan asked. Rex counted down from five before he said,

"Yeah, I'm okay."

The doorknob twisted, and Jordan appeared behind him in the mirror, wrapping his arms around his waist and dropping his chin on Rex's shoulder. "Thought maybe you fell in or something," he teased. Despite the nightmare of emotions shuddering inside of him, Rex smiled.

"Nope, just thinking."

"Penny for your thoughts?"

"Nothing exciting." Rex cleared his throat and turned back to Jordan, distracting him with a kiss. "C'mon. Let's get back to bed." He led Jordan out of the bathroom with his hands on his shoulders. When he reached back to flick off the light, he caught sight of himself in the mirror, and his forced smile faded.

Thirteen

Jordan didn't get nervous often. Alright, so maybe that was a lie, and he did have a tendency to stress over even the smallest of details. He couldn't help it. Anxiety was in his nature, and he rarely had the means to cope with it. Knowing himself, Jordan spent most of Saturday morning trying to think about anything else but the fact that Rex wasn't answering his phone and he wasn't texting him back.

He distracted himself with laundry, doing the dishes, and making sure the house was spotless for the meeting that was happening shortly. Busy work always cleared his head and kept him from going down a catastrophizing spiral that would leave him stressed for the rest of the morning. He even considered heading to the grocery store to try out a new recipe, like he did when things got too bad to handle, but it wasn't to that point yet.

Every now and then, though, Jordan found himself wiping his hands and reaching for his cellphone to see if Rex had responded. It wasn't like him to leave him hanging for this long. Usually, Rex had a message sent back before he could even put the phone down and do something else. That was how they'd gotten to know each other better in the middle of the night, back before Rex had become a regular member. He rarely got any sleep in when he and Rex started texting each other.

"Answer your phone, dummy," Jordan muttered, tossing his cellphone onto the couch in irritation. Whatever, he thought. He had more important things to worry about, like what he was going to serve for the treat during the meeting. He scrolled through his favorite baking blog, Made with Love, and settled on an easy chocolate-vanilla swirl cupcake recipe. He already had all the ingredients, and if he timed it right, he'd have them baked and iced just before the rest of the club members arrived.

Try as he might to get his mind off of Rex, he found his thoughts drifting back to their dinner last weekend. While he combined the butter and sugar, he grimaced at some of the things his father had said, and when he placed colorful cupcake liners in the baking tray, he rocked back and forth on his heels at the thought of growing up with a man like that in his life.

His relationship with his parents hadn't been the greatest, but they were never as strained as Rex, Amy, and Alan. Even at their worst, his folks still respected him enough not to talk to him the way Alan did. Hell, when he came out to Sherleen, she'd insulted his parents and him but had never crossed the line that far. She'd never gone far enough to permanently damage their relationships, and when she finally came around to acceptance, she put her all into making amends.

It felt foreign to be harboring so much antagonism to blood relatives, but Jordan didn't want to assume. He didn't know what it was like growing up with Alan. If he'd been anything like he was at the restaurant, Jordan was willing to bet that Rex's resentment towards the man was more than warranted.

Jordan had just finished icing the last cupcake when there was the first knock at the door. He wiped his hands and hurried to answer it, internally sighing when he saw that it wasn't Rex. Still, he met Charles with his usual enthusiasm, inviting him inside and keeping him entertained until the other members arrived.

"These look heavenly," Gloria said once they were all settled in the living room and the cupcakes were situated in the middle of the coffee table. "Did you make these?"

"I did," he smiled bashfully. "I made enough for everyone, but I don't think Rex is going to be able to make it this week, so if someone wants to take a few home, I don't think he'd mind too much."

"Shame that he couldn't make it," Madeline said, glancing at Jordan with knowing eyes. Jordan was both amused with her teasing and disappointed from his absence. It pained him to say it, but since Rex had been around, Meet Cute Club had felt different. More exciting. They had a new perspective, from a guy who'd grown up hating these kinds of books but was now willing and eager to talk about them.

He was what they needed, a single spark to rekindle their burning love for the club, and without him, things felt off, like they were missing a key component. Even with being so new, Rex had come in and shaken up even the way Jordan saw the club.

"Well, let's all get into it then, yeah?" He reached for his copy of the book they'd read, flipping through it. "So. That cliffhanger."

"Ugh," Madeline said, rolling her eyes. "I wish there had been a note or something in the front that said that this was a series! I was so looking forward to Darrek and Zane getting together and then bam, end of the book. The cliffhanger alone made me almost throw my Kindle across the room!"

"Those were my thoughts," Charles said, nodding enthusiastically. "I want them to make it through this, but the way she ended that last chapter? I don't know if there's any way for them to repair the damage and fall in love again!"

The club dove headfirst into the conversation about the way the author had ended the first book in what was apparently going to be a series. He personally preferred to start series when they were finished, that way he could binge them all, but Gloria didn't seem to mind that they'd have to wait for the next book.

"It gives me something to look forward to! People to root for, really," she said, shrugging.

"I just don't know how I feel about ending things so hopeless. I'm sure Krista will turn the story around in the next book, but I'm impatient," Jordan said, pouting.

After the meeting, Jordan helped his friends pack up their treats in small plastic containers, chattering about what he wanted to make for the next meeting. They buzzed with possibilities, and it made him that much more excited for the following Saturday. Charles was the first to leave, quickly followed by Madeline. Gloria stayed back to talk about other books they could read for next month's schedule, and he quickly wrote down the titles in his phone.

To his disappointment, there was still no message from

Rex. Not even an explanation as to why he hadn't shown up for Meet Cute Club.

"Everything okay, hon?" Gloria asked, lightly placing a hand on his forearm.

"Yeah, I'm fine!" He put on a bright smile and stuffed his phone into his pocket. "I'll make sure to see if they have these books at Millerstone next week."

"I'm so excited," she said, giving a small happy dance. Jordan laughed and grabbed her coat from the rack for her. Jordan walked Gloria to the front door, giving her a wave as she headed out to her car. Movement drew his attention to the curb across the street. Rex sat on his motorcycle, propped up like he'd been waiting there for a minute. As Jordan approached, he climbed off the bike and let down the kickstand.

"You're late," Jordan noted. There was no animosity in his voice when he continued, "How dare you."

"I wanted to come, but..." Rex's sentence trailed off, and he looked away, his eyes following Gloria as she drove home.

"What's wrong?" It was obvious whatever was on Rex's mind was bothering him. Very rarely did he miss the chance to shoot back at Jordan's light jests.

Rex pressed his lips together in a tight line before he looked back at Jordan. "I... I don't know how to say it, so

I'll just say it. I'm not really into the club very much these days."

"Shut up," Jordan laughed, rolling his eyes. When Rex's serious expression didn't break into a grin like it always did when he was joking, Jordan's face fell. "You're for real?"

"Yeah."

"I—why?"

This didn't make sense. Just a few days ago, Rex was leading book discussions and getting excited about what they were scheduled to read next month. Now, out of nowhere, the club wasn't for him and he wasn't all that interested in it anymore? That didn't sound like Rex at all.

"I'm just being honest here. I'm not into this whole romance thing like I thought I was."

The way he said it, Jordan wasn't sure whether he was talking about the books or what was going on between the two of them. "I don't get it. You know you like the club, Rex."

"I don't, Jordan. I thought I did, but it feels like I'm wasting my time. I have shit to do. I have someone interested in buying the house. I'm still not even done cleaning out everything inside of it, and I can't keep letting you and the club distract me."

Jordan's throat squeezed tight. "I didn't realize this was all such an inconvenience."

"It's not your fault. It's mine. I should've never gotten involved in any of this." He gestured to both Jordan and his house. "I knew I wouldn't be here long, but I still went with it. That was a dick move on my part. But now I have a buyer, and when the house goes, so will I. Sweet Rose is...it's not for me. There's nothing here for me in this town. Nothing and no one."

It felt cruel to say these things to Jordan, like telling a kid Santa wasn't real or building up someone's hope only to let them down. The truth was, it was easier to tell Jordan that he was just leaving town than it was to admit that he himself was aware that he'd never be enough. He wasn't the "cinnamon roll" everyone in Meet Cute Club talked about.

He was an asshole. He was a coward who knew he would only be wasting Jordan's time and effort, were he to stick around. He was his father's son, and no matter how far he ran or how often he cursed the man, they shared similarities that he would never be able to shake. Indivisibly tied by the tainted blood that ran in both their veins.

"Is this because of what Amy said?" Jordan asked softly. "The boyfriend stuff? I was only joking when I repeated what she said."

"What? God, no," Rex groaned. "I just can't do this anymore, Jordan. I have to focus on what I'm doing. What we had was fun, but it's time for both of us to be serious.

I'm not a good guy, and you'll never get the happily ever after you get in all of your stupid books."

That seemed to do the trick. With agonizing satisfaction, Rex watched Jordan's demeanor change. That painful look on his face cracked, revealing anger beneath the surface.

"I see," Jordan said. Without another word, he turned and headed back to the house. When Rex grabbed his arm, Jordan jerked back, pointing a finger in his face. "Don't touch me."

"I—"

"Get the fuck away from me, Rex. Since you don't want to be here, go! Run away like you said you would. Like your dad said you would. I knew you were an asshole, but I didn't think you were this cold-hearted."

"Jordan…"

"You made me actually care about you, and then you tell me it never happened. That's awesome, Rex. Really, thank you so much for wasting two months of my life that I could've been focusing on this club. Thank you for reminding me once again why these books are only fairy tales. For a second, I was starting to think one of those endings would happen for me."

Jordan choked back a wave of tears, focusing on his anger instead. Rex had come into his life out of nowhere, swearing up and down that he would give this all a chance.

Pretending he was worth any of the effort.

"Since you think this club is so stupid and none of it matters, don't come crawling back here when you realize how much you miss me, Rex. I'll mail your grandma's books back to you."

Rex sighed. "Keep them."

"I don't want them. You can donate them yourself. Or just throw them away like the trash you think they are."

Rex stood with his hands in his pocket, jaw clenched tight as he fought back the urge to say anything else. Jordan deserved to get all this out. He was right. Rex *had* wasted his time, and these verbal slaps were well-deserved. Still, the shame and guilt made him want to die right there on the spot. Seeing Jordan this torn up drove his instincts to pull the man in his arms and apologize.

But he couldn't. This had to be final. After he sold the house, he'd be gone. Entertaining the idea that he and Jordan could be together would only make things that much worse when he inevitably fled Sweet Rose one night, months, maybe even years, from now.

"Why are you still standing here?" Jordan asked. "You're leaving, right? Don't let me hold you up."

"Yeah," was all Rex could get out of his hoarse throat.

"Cool. Now leave. And don't come back, you hear me? Don't come back."

A second later, Jordan slammed the front door closed. Rex pressed the heels of his hands against his eyes, fighting back the scream bubbling up in his throat. "Fuck," he whispered when really, he just wanted to shout. To yell at himself for fucking things up so monumentally. For being the one to have to do this for both of them.

The selfish part of him wanted to bang on the door and apologize. Pull Jordan to his chest and kiss away his tears and tell him that he was stupid for ever thinking he could leave like this. But this was a blessing. A bandage pulled off swiftly, a sharp bit of pain to spare something much more prolonged in the future. He could only hope that if he ever spoke to him again, Jordan would understand why he'd done this. He'd find someone worthy of the unfettered, unabashed joy that Jordan brought the people around him.

Rather than sticking around any longer, Rex grabbed his bike and headed out.

Jordan watched from the window, relieved and heartbroken to see him throw a leg over the motorcycle, start up the engine, and pull away from the curb. Rex was really gone.

The words didn't quite make sense to him. They were still fresh, foreign in a way. Jordan stood still as a statue in the window, his mind racing and his stomach twisting. The cupcakes from earlier soured in his belly, and he felt the overwhelming urge to throw up. He wanted to grab all of the books from his shelf and toss them to the street. He'd tricked himself into thinking any of that joy was real, that one day, a man like one of the leads would walk into his life and show him that he was worthy of love.

He swiped at the wetness prickling his eyes, laughing bitterly.

"Stupid," he said, his laugh quieting, wavering until he stopped fighting back the tears. He stood in the window, face held in his hands, body racked with sobs. Despite the forest fire of rage in his stomach, what he wanted more than anything was for Rex to just come back.

Jordan knew he wouldn't.

Fourteen

Jordan woke before he opened his eyes, and rather than rolling out of bed like he did every other morning, he lay still, listening to the repetitive tick-tock of the clock hanging on his wall. It was steady, never missing a beat. He kept his eyes closed, trying his hardest to let the sound lull him back to sleep. Things were more pleasant in his dreams. Even the nightmares.

As hard as he tried, though, he couldn't drift off again. He was cursed with consciousness, forced to finally open his eyes and stare up at the blank white ceiling. When he turned to face the clock, he felt a jolt. Nearly ten o'clock on a Saturday, and he was just now waking up. Any other weekend, he'd be in a panic, running around trying to get ready before the meeting. This morning, he couldn't find the strength to care.

He could barely muster up the energy to roll over and grab his phone from the nightstand. There, he found two missed calls from Charles, as well as a few texts from the other members.

Is the club meeting today?

Jordan?

Hello?

He couldn't do it.

For a moment, he considered strong-arming himself into crawling to the shower, but what was the point? If he wasn't going to be as enthusiastic as he usually was, they might as well all stay home. The remaining three club members deserved better than that.

Three.

That was all he had left. When he'd first met Rex, he was at least making things work, but now two were gone, and he was sure that soon, the others would follow. Rather than watching helplessly, he decided then and there that he'd say something.

No meeting today, he texted back, then put the phone on silent and tossed it to the floor.

He knew shortly the phone would be blowing up with calls, everyone asking what was wrong and why he hadn't responded sooner. It was shitty to leave them all hanging, but what was shittier was the fact that despite all the texts he'd received, none of them had been from Rex. By now, Jordan had expected the man to come crawling back, begging and pleading for forgiveness. He'd have eventually realized how big of a mistake it was to dump him and the club.

But Rex was gone. He was really gone, not just "I'm making a bad decision and I'll regret this soon enough" gone. Jordan knew he'd have better luck trying to turn water to wine than get a response from Rex. The thought made his chest ache and his stomach sink, but he refused to cry anymore. Crying achieved nothing, and it only made him exhausted afterwards. The best thing would be to do something to get his mind off Rex's absence.

Fill the empty holes in his schedule with people he cared about.

Sherleen.

She was the reason he tossed aside his covers and nearly dragged himself to the shower to clean up. As shameful as it was to admit, Jordan hadn't showered since his job interview on Tuesday afternoon. There'd been no reason to since he'd stayed firmly planted in bed, head buried under his pillow as he fought off every little reminder of Rex.

He couldn't even stomach looking at his bookshelf downstairs. It took all his mental fortitude not to swipe the shelves clean and toss every last romance book in the trash. He didn't care about his collection anymore. Somehow, Rex had wormed his way into the one safe haven Jordan had, a parasite in what he'd once considered paradise.

Though he wanted nothing more than to get rid of the books, he refused to let someone have that power over him. He'd been in love with love before Rex had ever stepped foot in his life. Now that he was gone, he wouldn't let Rex take this piece of joy with him on his way out. Not after all the hours he'd put into the club, and the years he'd spent, nose deep in the pages of every book in his collection.

After his shower, he pulled a baggy hoodie and jeans on, grabbing his phone from the floor and dialing Sherleen's number. She answered immediately, eager to go shopping with him at McDaniel's Grocery. She was in desperate need of some of her favorite Minute Maid juice, and she wouldn't stop bugging him until he agreed to take her.

Waiting in his car outside of the nursing home, Jordan glanced to his left. Only a block away stood the towering building he'd had his interview at. The place was incredibly stuffy, and he wasn't going to be much more than a glorified secretary for Snapdragon Energy. The company wasn't much, just a smaller corporation that provided power to a section of Sweet Rose, but it was better than nothing. Being proactive gave him something to do other than wallow away in his emotions, and it didn't hurt that he'd finally have another job.

"Hey, baby," Sherleen said as she put her walker in the back of his car. She closed the back door and climbed into the passenger's seat, reaching over to give his hand a squeeze. "You look good. How you been?"

He forced a smile and shrugged. "I've been."

"It'll be okay, Jordan."

He desperately wanted to believe it, even to the point that he was willing to ignore the fact that people couldn't just walk out of lives without leaving an impact. If possible, he would've deluded himself to help ease the pain. But that wasn't the kind of person he was. He was realistic, and realistically, this would take time. How long, he wasn't certain, but he knew for a fact that these things never ended as painlessly as people hoped.

"Let's go," he said, changing the subject and pulling away from the curb. Sherleen's somber brown eyes examined him, but thankfully, she said nothing.

Saturdays seemed to be the busiest at McDaniel's, which was fine by Jordan. The more time he spent out of the house and around other people, the better. He followed Sherleen up and down the aisles shopping for groceries, only slipping away to pick up a few things he needed for himself. He stepped up to the deli to find Tony behind the counter like usual.

"There the kid is," he said with a toothy smile. "I was starting to wonder where you were at."

"Last week got busy," Jordan lied, trying his damnedest to keep his voice chipper. "Can I get the usual?"

"Honey-baked and cheddar, coming up."

Jordan pushed his cart over to the lobster tank nearby, leaning forward to watch as the creatures all scuttled over one another. He found them to be quite creepy-looking, but in the kind of way he could never stop staring at. But like all things lately, watching the crustaceans immediately made him think of what Rex had ordered at the restaurant.

Internally groaning, he thanked Tony for his order and headed off to find his grandmother. Much to his disappointment, she stood in the book section, flipping through a paperback that had just arrived. He approached apprehensively, holding back the urge to roll his eyes at all the happy couples embracing on the covers.

"This one looks interesting," Sherleen said, holding up a book with a Black couple. "I don't know when they started putting us on the front of these, but I like it."

"Wasn't too long ago, unfortunately."

"Well, I say you read this for your next meeting. He's a cop, and she's the sole witness to a murder that took place in the wealthy part of town. And apparently, he's got all kinds of Southern charm."

"Honestly, I don't know if I'm even doing the club anymore."

The smile on Sherleen's face fell, and she put a hand on her hip. "What are you talking about?"

"Nobody cares anymore, Grandma. People keep leaving, and I really just don't give a damn about these books anymore."

The way she narrowed her eyes at him made Jordan shift on his feet and look away, far too uncomfortable to deal with her menacing glare. "Jordan, stop playing with me. This is all you talk about. You're not going to give it all up just because some boy said he didn't want to be part of it anymore."

"It's not just that," he said with exasperation. Yes, it was a sizeable chunk, but that wasn't the only reason. "I can't keep wasting my time reading these things. First of all, it gets expensive having to buy five paperbacks every week."

"You don't have to buy that many, you *want* to."

"*Anyway*," he said, moving past her interjection. "I've been looking for jobs, too. I have a second interview with Snapdragon tomorrow, and I really think I could have that secured. I don't have time to be wasting on stupid stories that all end the same. I'd rather spend my time doing something productive."

Sherleen's lips pulled into a flat line, and she put the book back on the shelf. "Hm."

God. Jordan knew that "hm." When she had nothing nice to say, Sherleen would often respond with a simple "hm" and get back to business. He wanted to insist that this was a good thing, but he doubted she would listen. Her mind was already made up.

Whether she liked it or not, Jordan knew he had to hang it up for now. It was time to be an adult and drop the hopeless romantic act, at least until he was once more employed and able to afford spending so much on books that pitched a fantasy to him that he was certain wouldn't come true.

"If there's anything else you need to know about the place, please don't hesitate to call me, Jalisa," Rex said, grabbing his pen and underlining a few important details he'd need to remember.

He'd been on the phone with Jalisa for the past half hour going over everything involving a potential buyer. The house was nearly finished, save for a few boxes up in the attic that he planned on tackling after the call. Soon, this house would be gone, and with it, all of the memories.

It was bittersweet in a way, really. Rex had never been the kind of person that found places or objects sentimental.

In his mind, those things could be taken away or lost. He placed importance on experiences rather than tokens. He couldn't lose an experience once he went through it, and he would always be able to come back to it in his mind.

That's why it was surprising how down he felt about the idea of someone else living in Nana Bailey's home. She'd owned it for forty years before she passed away. His father had been raised in the house, and when things between him and Alan got bad, he was also raised here. It felt like giving up a piece of their history.

Alan didn't want the house, though. Rex didn't need it. Not when he had plans to leave and travel the country again. Amy was just starting her life in a new apartment for the first time, and his mother had only recently finished payments on her own home. Nobody *needed* Nana Bailey's home the same way they all had years ago.

That was the part that struck him the hardest. She was really gone, and they were moving on without her. It felt wrong in a way. She'd done her part in raising not one but two generations, and somehow, selling the home felt like giving up all her hard work. As tempting as it was to head down that road, Rex cleared his throat and finished up his conversation with his real estate agent.

"Sounds great. I'll contact you tomorrow with some more information about the buyer, how does that work for you?" she asked.

"Perfect. And if you can't reach me, you have my email as well."

After the call, Rex leaned back in his seat and looked around the kitchen. The room was as empty as every other room in the house, minus the air mattress he slept on upstairs. After the nightmare of last Saturday, he'd gone into a state of hyperfocus, burying himself in work to get his mind off of Jordan. The sooner he got the hell out of dodge, the easier this would all be.

Almost reluctantly, Rex climbed the stairs to the second storey of the house, then a separate staircase that led to the attic. In the left corner of the room stood a few large boxes that he needed to finish, but after that, he'd be free.

He made easy work inspecting the largest boxes. Each of them contained baby clothes and some of the toys he and Amy left behind when they spent summers at the house. He pulled a worn-down action figure from inside and smiled, wiping away the dust on his face with his thumb. If Rex thought hard enough, he could still hear the way Amy would make him play with dolls despite their sizeable age gap. He always made an exception for her, but only after Nana encouraged him to spend time with her.

"She's the only sister you've got," he said aloud, thinking back to her favorite phrase. "You better cherish her before it's too late."

He tossed the toy back into the box and scooted it aside, squatting down to open the smaller one beside it. Beneath albums and albums of photos of her as a child up until she was in her eighties, Rex found an unmarked leather book. He flipped through it curiously, and when he began to read it, it was obvious this had been one of Nana's journals.

Amongst all of her other hobbies, writing was something the woman had done frequently. Not a night went by that she hadn't put her thoughts on paper, retelling her day to a book that no one would ever read. Well, no one other than Rex.

Most of the book appeared to be quite uneventful, but as he approached September, he realized where he was in time. His parents had just split, and though Alan always hated it, Nana Bailey had taken him and Phoebe in. The entries grew noticeably longer as Rex continued to read, and rather than giving general overviews of her day, Nana Bailey dug deep.

She spoke about Alan like she had faith in him. No matter how terrible he was, she'd always yearned for him to make the right decision. It both incensed Rex and shattered his heart that she never lost hope in Alan. No matter how many times he fucked up, she was always there to cheer him on and tell him to do better. Make better decisions.

"I just don't want Rexy to see any of this," she'd written sometime in August. *"He's not that old, but I can see it on his face. He may not understand all the details about Phoebe and Alan's situation, but he knows something is wrong. Watching his parents fight can't be good for him, I don't think."*

Rex stopped reading and looked away, flooded with memories of the shouting matches his parents got into. All the nights Alan had shown up at Nana's home, drunk off his ass, demanding that Phoebe give him back his son. The times he cried in his mother's arms, begging her to go back to Alan and not understanding why she wouldn't make the family whole again.

He understood now. She'd fought for years to keep things together, but it was Alan that had ruined everything. He had a knack for that the same way Rex did.

"I'm worried that if they don't figure this out, Rexy won't ever get to see what a healthy relationship looks like. They say that can happen when a child witnesses a nasty divorce. They get so used to fighting and anger that they think love is like that. The only thing that could break my heart more than what Alan's done is if Rexy suffers from it too. I can't let him think love isn't real, or that it means always being hurt."

"Nana," he whispered, pressing his fingers hard against the aged pages of the journal. He traced the cursive letters, grounding himself. But that wasn't what brought his emotions past the point he could control them. It was the rest of the entry, the way Nana Bailey swore to herself that she would spend every second of every day showing Rex what love looked like that had him dotting the pages of her diary with his tears. How she went into detail in nearly every entry about all the ways she'd do it. Spending time with him and Amy. Taking him down to the library and reading for hours with him. Making sure he knew that he would always have her heart.

He'd always been blind to it, or assumed that was just what grandmothers did. They spoiled their grandchild rotten because they didn't have to be around them at their worst. But not Nana. She'd been there through it all, every bitter fight and broken dish, determined to show him that it was all worth it.

It wasn't all bullshit the way Rex had assumed. Maybe his father was incapable of seeing it, but Rex could see it perfectly. He knew what love looked like. He knew what kind of sacrifice it took. The strength needed to promise someone that no matter how rough the future for them might get, they would bear it all together.

All she'd wanted was for him to find love, to find someone to care about the way she cared for him, and he'd utterly, royally fucked it all up. Rex considered himself relatively intelligent, but in this particular moment, he felt so goddamn stupid.

He pulled his phone from his pocket and dialed Amy like muscle memory. Just like he assumed something was wrong whenever she called, Amy answered the phone with a wary, "Rex? What's wrong?"

"I need your help, Ames. I screwed up really fucking bad."

Fifteen

"So, let me get this straight… He didn't tell none of y'all why we're over here so goddamn early in the morning?" Omar asked.

"No! All he told me was that he needed my help, and to call everyone else up and see if they were willing to help too." Amy seemed just as confused as the rest of them. Rex couldn't blame them. He'd been a bit vague when he told Amy that he needed her help. All he'd said was that he'd screwed up with Jordan and desperately needed to fix the situation. That was more than enough for her, given how invested in their…relationship she was. Well, what relationship they'd once had.

Rex hadn't been able to sleep a bit since he'd found Nana's journal, his mind racing with all the ways he could fix this. He spent nights tossing and turning, and his nightmares were all about Jordan rejecting him each time he tried to apologize. It was clear that he had to do something big. Something to show Jordan that he saw how wrong he was, how confused he'd been. It was a stupid mistake, leaving him like that, and now he was willing to jump out of a plane without a parachute if it meant earning his forgiveness.

That was why he carried two giant handfuls of flyers outside to his front porch where all of his friends were. Omar looked like he'd just rolled out of bed, as well as Amy, Lana, and Charles, but Gloria and Madeline were dressed to the nines. Of course, the two morning birds would show up looking as beautiful as ever.

"There he is," Amy said. "What the hell took you so long? I'm out here having to play damage control for everyone. Omar's pissed," she said in a hushed voice, looking over her shoulder.

"Omar's always pissed," Rex replied, raising his voice so the man could hear.

"Damn right. What are we even doing, man?"

"Well, Madeline told me that Jordan said Meet Cute Club was on hold indefinitely, and I'm not going to let that happen. It's my fault that he gave up hope on it. I ruined it when he and I…" He struggled to find the words, but thankfully—or unluckily in Rex's case—Amy seemed more than happy to fill in the gaps for the others.

"When he and Jordan broke up."

Gloria's eyes lit up as she said, "I knew it!"

Madeline nodded. "I figured that was what the problem was. You skipped the last meeting, and Gloria told me you were waiting for him outside afterwards. You fucked up big time, buddy. Like, huge. Honestly, I'd be surprised if Jordan ever looked at you again."

"Hey, Madeline?" Rex said.

"Hm?"

"You're not helping." Madeline cracked a bashful smile, and Rex held back a deep sigh. "I'm going to fix this, but I need all of your help. Omar, I know you and Amy don't care about this club, but you've met Jordan. You know how passionate he is about this stuff."

"Kind of nerdy," Omar muttered.

"Kind of?" Amy snorted.

Rex narrowed his eyes at both of them. "Amy, you collect anime figurines, and Omar has every Marvel movie in a glass case in his living room. Neither of you get to call anyone nerdy." That shut both of them up, if only for a moment. Then Amy nudged Lana and whispered,

"Look at him defending his boyfriend."

"It's so cute," Lana snickered.

Rex made it a point to ignore that comment, determined to get this ragtag group back in line. "Guys, this is serious. I need everyone to bring their A game today. Jordan is the one that brought us all together. He made this club and kept it running, even when he was terrified it was going to fizzle out for good. He spent hundreds of dollars baking, buying books, and making sure everything looked great for us. Omar, he promoted you when we were handing out flyers, and Amy, he gave you yet another thing to tease me about."

"I respect him for that," Amy said.

"We owe it to him to bring this club back from the dead. We need to go harder than before. I'm talking chasing people through back alleys trying to get them to agree to come to at least one meeting. Don't take no for an answer, you hear me? Asses in seats, that's what we need."

Omar gave another sigh, but took a chunk from the stack in Rex's left hand. "One day, I'mma get tired of saving your little ass whenever you screw up," he said.

"But today's not that day," Rex remarked. He divvied up the rest of the flyers between the five people on his porch, then checked the time on his phone. "We'll split up and section off the town. Three on East Sweet Rose and four on West. West is bigger, so we'll need an extra person to help with that. It's eight right now, so we'll meet back up at my house at noon for lunch. If we still need to hand out more flyers, then that's what we'll do, okay? Sound good?"

"Sounds great," Madeline said, hand on her hip. "I want the OG members of Meet Cute Club."

"Perfect," Rex said. It would be easier for them to all work together since they'd known each other the longest. Omar and Amy were still strangers, and he would have a better chance of keeping them all in line than anyone else in the club.

"Let's fucking do this," Lana said, clapping loudly and heading back to her car. The rest of the group split up and headed off. Amy and Omar stayed on the porch with Rex, where she said,

"We can all take my car. I don't think we'll all fit on the back of Rex's motorcycle."

"Not unless both of y'all wanna sit in my lap," Omar muttered.

When Amy smirked and opened her mouth, Rex splayed his fingers and planted his hand on her face. "Don't you even start, brat," he said. She laughed and followed the two to her car, sliding into the driver's seat and buckling up.

With everyone as hyped up as he could get them, Rex was only now starting to feel the pressure of this. He had so much to do, so many miracles to pull off, to get back in Jordan's good graces. He knew apologies were one thing, but the best apology was action, and dammit, he was going to do something about Meet Cute Club's indefinite pause.

This wasn't all, though. Handing out flyers and getting the word out there was one thing, but when the others finally took a long look at the papers in their hands, they'd see the small alterations he'd made to the location where the club met, and more than that, there was an added line at the bottom that he knew would come as a surprise to all of them.

He had to go all out.

Jordan deserved his romance novel finale, the moment where all eyes were on him as Rex bared his soul and groveled at his feet for forgiveness. For anyone else, he would've scoffed at the idea. What did he look like, embarrassing himself like that? He was Rex fucking Bailey. But when it came to Jordan, he was Rhett, who now knew what love looked like and refused to let his own baggage get in the way of something he and Jordan both deserved.

He didn't care if he had to go on live TV and make a statement.

He was getting his man back.

If there was one thing Jordan was fantastic at, it was slipping into routines. Back in the day, his school counselor told him that he had a special talent for finding his niche and sticking to it. Routines were easy for him. They required little to no thinking, and at times, it felt almost automated. Working at Snapdragon Energy had become that for him.

In the week and a half that he'd been working the front desk, he'd already put together a simple routine. He sat down, took a long sip of his coffee, logged into his computer, slipped on his headset, and checked his emails. There were never any emails for him, of course, but he still liked to check, just in case. It was basic, nothing that was all too impressive, but going through the movements prepared him for the day, however uneventful it would be.

"Morning, Jordan," a woman named Lydia said as she breezed past him. Not very many employees at the company said a word to him this early in the day, so he appreciated her kindness more than she probably knew.

"Morning!"

At first, Jordan had anticipated being treated the same way he had at the call center. His managers had somehow found a way to make him feel completely irrelevant and imperatively integral to the company all at once. He was led to believe that his absence would mean nothing and everything at the same time. But Snapdragon was actually quite pleasant.

The environment was nice and clean, the people were friendly once they'd all had their coffee IV drips, and the pay was substantially better than what he was making at the last place he'd worked. Sure, things got a little lonely, but the computer at his front desk was loaded with stock games like Minesweeper, as well as Candy Crush and Subway Surfers. When no one was around, he secretly opened up one of the games and entertained himself between phone calls.

At the call center, he used to fill his free time up with reading, but since he'd stopped doing meetings for Meet Cute Club, there was really no point. He needed other hobbies, things that didn't fill his head with fantasies most men would never live up to. He needed to be *realistic*. The Jordan from a few months ago would've scoffed at the idea, but this one? His perspective had changed, thanks to Rex.

Denying himself the self-pitying pleasure of wallowing at the thought of Rex, Jordan zoned in on work, going through his calendar to organize all of his boss's meetings once again. Administrative assistance was much more his speed. He didn't have to deal with angry customers cursing him out or throwing slurs in his face, nor did he feel the same pressure of keeping Snapdragon afloat. They needed each other equally.

At lunch, Jordan hung around the small rec room in the back of the building, stirring his cup of noodles while he listened to his coworkers talk about how one of their spouses had ruined her birthday by not mentioning it until nearly eleven o'clock that night. Lydia brushed a strand of blonde hair behind her ear and turned to Jordan.

"What do you think, Jordan? Should Felicia forgive him for what he did?"

He didn't know these two ladies all that well, but not wanting to seem standoffish, he said, "I'd probably give him the silent treatment for a few days."

"That's what I'm saying," Lydia exclaimed. "Remind him why you deserved to have a good birthday. If he actually cares about you, he'll find some way to make it up to you."

Felicia sighed and picked at her microwavable fettuccini. "I guess. I'm just worried that if I do anything too harsh, he'll be the one upset with me."

"Men are trash that way," Lydia conceded.

Lydia had no idea how deeply Jordan related to that sentiment. Were he closer with these ladies, he probably would've commiserated with them about all their relationship woes, but because he still felt new to the team, he remained relatively quiet, nodding when appropriate and keeping up with their conversation from a distance.

"So, Jordan, why did you pick Snapdragon? Most of our staff here is a bit older. Doesn't really seem like something a younger guy would be interested in," Felicia said, turning to him.

"Honestly? I needed the money and couldn't afford to

be picky," he said, cracking a smile that the other two women mirrored. "Also, I'm pretty good with older people. Sometimes I like them a lot more than guys my age."

"Ugh, an old soul. I love that," Lydia said, reaching out to pat his shoulder. "I think it'll be a nice change of pace to see a guy out in the front of the office. Especially one so handsome."

Jordan glanced at the wedding ring on her finger, then back up at her with curiosity. When she followed his line of sight, she blushed. "Don't tell my wife I said that, okay? God, do you remember the last time Shauna came up here when she thought I was stepping out on her?"

This launched another ten-minute conversation about Lydia's marriage, and thankfully, it put him at ease. The last thing he needed when dealing with a broken heart was a smitten coworker and an even angrier wife barging through the lobby doors.

After they finished their food, Jordan returned to his desk and flipped through a book he'd brought with him. It felt weird reading something other than a book about lusty maidens and mafia dons with uncomfortably high sex drives, but he wanted to branch out. Test out other genres and see what else was out there besides the books he'd been obsessed with since he was a kid.

Jordan was so engrossed in the domestic thriller that he

almost didn't notice the front doors open when someone entered the lobby carrying the largest rose bouquet he'd ever seen. The person approached the desk, clearly unable to see, but when they plopped it down, they stuck their head out from the side of the roses, and Jordan nearly died on the spot.

No fucking way.

"Delivery for Jordan Collins," the older Black woman said, pushing the bridge of her ruby red glasses higher on her broad nose. She smiled at him like she knew *he* knew exactly who she was.

"P-Patricia?"

"Jordan?"

"Yes, yes. Oh my god, yes. What are you doing here? Is this real?" Jordan was sure he'd slipped and hit his head in the shower, and this was all a long, elaborate fantasy. There was no other explanation as to why Patricia *thee* Hayes was standing in front of him holding an oversized floral arrangement.

"This is very real," she chuckled.

"Okay, but why?" He didn't mean to be rude, but the excitement in his stomach overrode his manners. Were Sherleen around, she would surely pop him in the mouth and tell him to show some damn respect. "Sorry, I'm just— I don't—"

"That's okay, don't apologize. I think if you read that letter right there, it might all make a little more sense." Patricia pointed one perfectly-shaped white oval nail at the tiny pink envelope nestled in the stems of the roses.

Almost too stunned to comprehend what she was not-so-subtly hinting at, Jordan snapped out of it long enough to reach forward and grab the envelope. Inside, he found a letter written in a tall, scratchy script that he recognized. Only Rex could have such a pretty face and such ugly penmanship.

"You said don't come back, so I sent someone else in my place. I'm not done apologizing. Ask Patricia what's next."

It was cryptic and left Jordan both restless and eager to know what the hell they were going to do next. The pride in him wanted to tear the card up and tell Rex to shove all twelve roses up his ass, but somehow, some way, Rex had sent him flowers delivered by the one person in his life he loved more than his grandmother.

Whatever kind of black magic Rex had done to get this woman here, Jordan wasn't going to let it go to waste. Not with Patricia standing in front of him, smiling knowingly.

"Um… What's next?" he asked, doing exactly as Rex's note said.

"Well, there's a car waiting outside for both of us. I'm not allowed to tell you where it's going, but I can say that you probably won't want to miss it. Will you ride with me, Jordan?"

Hearing his favorite author say his name was nearly enough to make Jordan faint right there, but he kept his composure and nodded, practically jumping from his seat. "I have to ask my boss if I can leave early."

"Don't bother. Rex already called him this morning. All you have to do is ride with me."

Every last word she spoke came out so eloquently, so perfect that Jordan was more than willing to sit there and listen to her read the phonebook, or even just the incredibly dull emails sitting in his boss's inbox. Instead, he grabbed his jacket and pulled it on, snagging the large vase of flowers as well. Suddenly, he stopped in his place and turned to her.

"Can I hug you? If not, I understand, I just—"

Patricia's hug shut him right up. She squeezed her arms around him and filled his nose with the smell of her rose and vanilla lotion. Right then and there, he decided that no hug would ever come close to this.

Nobody in the world could hold a candle to Patricia, and he was willing to throw himself on the sword to protect her.

"You're so cute, you know that?" she asked, stepping back to cup his cheek. "C'mon. We don't want to keep this Rex fellow waiting any longer than we already have. Something tells me every second we're gone is eating him alive."

"Between you and me, let him squirm."

Her thin brows went up. "Ooh, someone in the dog house?"

"He's sleeping on the couch in the dog house," he laughed.

"You're gonna have to tell me everything on the way there," she replied, walking to the door. Jordan hurried after to her, speeding up to get the door for her. When they made it to the street, a simple black Honda sat waiting for them. The driver nodded as the two of them climbed inside.

"Take us to..." Patricia's gaze slid to Jordan, and she smiled conspiratorially. "Take us to this address, please." She typed something on her phone and turned it to the driver, and he nodded.

"I know exactly the place. Buckle up," the driver replied.

Jordan followed instructions, stretching his belt across his chest and locking it in. He was suddenly thankful for the weighty vase in his lap, because if it weren't there, he was sure Patricia would be able to see his knees bouncing up and down nervously.

Whatever was going on, Rex had certainly gone all out. Jordan could only hope it would all lead to something positive, unlike the last time they'd spoken.

Sixteen

No matter how many different ways Jordan tried to worm information out of Patricia, she gave him no hints about where they were going. Not even the driver slipped up and spilled the beans. Frustrated but amused, Jordan sat back in his seat and stared out the window. He watched the town around him zip by, completely lost until they turned up on a hill and it suddenly hit him.

"Riverside Library," he said.

Patricia blinked, and a second later, she smiled.

"I'm right, aren't I? That's where we're headed?"

"You're not getting a word out of me, mister," she said, making a show of zipping her lips and tossing the key out the window. Jordan didn't need her confirmation, though. Something told him that they were headed up to the old library. For what? He had no damn idea. All he knew was that it made complete sense for Patricia Hayes to be taking him to the library.

When they pulled up to Riverside, Patricia climbed out first and gestured for Jordan to follow her. He held the bouquet close to his chest and walked in after her. The building was much louder than it had been when Rex brought him here, and when they stepped into one of the conference rooms in the back of the library, he saw why.

Rows and rows of chairs filled the center of the room, and at least fifty people looked their way when they passed through the doors. At the front of the room stood an easel with a large poster of Patricia's headshot, and beside that, a long table with a plush chair, stacks of her latest release, and a microphone. To the left of the table was a smartly-dressed Black woman with long braids. Jordan could only assume she worked with Patricia, perhaps as a publicist.

When the audience saw Jordan and Patricia, they burst into applause. She gave a wave to the group and pulled Jordan in for a quick hug. "There's a seat up front just for you," she said. After that, she hurried to take her seat behind the table. Jordan set the vase beside the door and hurried to the front, still in shock at what was going on. Just as Patricia said, there was an empty chair next to Sherleen, and he hurried to sit next to her.

"What are you doing here?" he whispered, looking around.

"That boyfriend of yours told me Miss Hayes was gonna be here, and I told all my orderlies to get the hell out the way so I can see my favorite author," she snickered.

"Sorry we're late, everybody," Patricia said into the microphone. "They don't call me romance's Lauryn Hill for nothing, right?"

The room filled with laughter, and Jordan eased back into his seat, spotting Rex across the room standing. He gave Jordan a quick nod, then pointed at Patricia as if to say, "pay attention." Obeying the wordless command, he turned his gaze back to the woman of the hour.

"Anyway, I wanted to first start off by thanking everyone for being here today. It's not every day that I get to meet readers, and it's always so humbling to know that people care enough to come out and talk to me. I'd also like to thank Rhett Bailey for taking care of my flight and the hotel room. He's organized one of the easiest bookings I've ever had, and I'm tempted to see if he wants to do this for me full-time."

Hearing Patricia talk about her storytelling process was like getting a Masterclass session for a skill Jordan was never going to use. He relished in all the tips and tricks she gave the audience, knowing full well that he didn't have the chops to be a writer. He was much more comfortable obsessing over the beautiful creations that came out of her head.

She was a natural up in the front too, expertly answering questions audience members had and giving useful pointers for anyone looking to publish books.

"Now that we're in the 21st century, there's no one to tell you what you can't write. If you want to write about giant blue aliens that want to sleep with gorgeous humans, you can. If you want to write about marginalized people that a lot of publishers would turn their nose up at, you can. Hell, if I'd had access to self-publishing, I'd have gotten my books out there five years sooner," she said.

Jordan's heart broke at the thought of all the wonderful stories he could've added to his library had publishers not blocked those ideas from hitting the shelves. After answering questions about publishing, she swung back around to her next book. When Jordan got to ask his question, he sat upright.

"The only question I have is, when are Claudia and Darren going to finally stop fighting each other and realize they were made for one another?"

A few attendees called out in agreement, wondering the same thing.

Patricia laughed softly. "Well, my publisher is going to kill me for this, but I'll say this: while the drama certainly isn't over for the two of them, the next book in the series will finally see our leads making things a little more official."

"A literal goddess," Jordan groaned, speaking without thinking. Sherleen patted his shoulder as she laughed, and Patricia gave him a shy smile.

Jordan hadn't been to many author appearances before, but the one thing he was certain of was that not a single one of them could hold a candle to the experience of meeting Patricia Hayes. She exceeded all of his expectations and proved his decade of dedication to be well worth it. After signing all the books brought up to her, she grabbed the microphone one last time.

"Today has been amazing, everybody. Sometimes, when you're fighting against deadlines and downing coffee, you forget why you even started doing this in the first place. You lose your mind in a way. But being here today… It's like a refresher course in why I do this. Why I tell these stories. I get to meet so many people. People I never would've assumed might care about my characters." Patricia shot a pointed glance Rex's way.

"But I'm so glad that I get to have these opportunities. I'm so glad that people are still reading not just my books, but all of romance. Despite all our flaws, this community is beautiful and diverse, and it taps into an emotion so many of us have. We just want to be loved, and to fall in love with love. That's why I've decided that for the next year, I'm going to be footing the bill for all the books Meet Cute Club will be reading."

Jordan choked on his spit. "What?"

Patricia grinned and continued. "If Meet Cute Club needs to rent a venue for meetings, I'll cover that. Rather than Jordan spending his money on books himself, I'll cover that, too. Anything the club needs, I want to take care of it as a thank you for reminding me why I do this *thing*. And Jordan, you will be getting a personal acknowledgement in my next novel."

If finding out about Patricia's generosity towards the club wasn't enough, the idea of being mentioned in her next book had him in tears seconds after registering what she said. The audience burst into applause once again, and Sherleen pulled him in for a hug. Jordan couldn't keep from crying. All the endless nights he'd spent worrying about the future of the club, and now Patricia was here telling everyone that they wouldn't need to spend a dime to be part of it.

When the excitement swelled to its peak and the signing was officially over, Patricia encouraged anyone that wanted a picture with her to come to the opposite side of the conference room so they could take them. Jordan felt like a snotty, teary mess, but thankfully, none of the other guests seemed to mind all that much. As he wiped his eyes and walked across the room to Rex, he was met with nothing but understanding smiles and comforting squeezes to his shoulders. He saw the familiar faces of people he never would've imagined stopping by. This had yet to sink in, and he remained suspended in reality, floating in the surrealism.

When he reached Rex, he couldn't say anything. He'd planned on a smartass comment or giving him a bit of shit for their fight weeks ago, but it was physically impossible. The only thing he could do was throw his arms around Rex and take in his familiar smell. He'd longed to inhale it just one more time, and now he finally could.

"I'm sorry, Jordan," Rex said low enough so that only Jordan could hear him. All eyes might've been on the two of them, but only Jordan needed to hear those words. If he could tear out his heart and turn it around so that the other man could see just how shitty he felt, he'd do it in…well, a heartbeat. There wasn't enough stress that he could put on it, not enough words to emphasize all the ways he felt sick for nearly destroying everything Jordan had worked to build.

"I'm sorry," he repeated, squeezing him closer. "I'm so fucking sorry, Jordan."

Jordan pulled back and cupped his face. "Stop apologizing, weirdo," he said, laughing through his tears.

"I'm just... Fuck, I was so stupid. I thought that running away would keep you from getting more hurt. I let my dad get in my head and convince me that I was just like him. But I'm not. I'm not leaving you. I'm not running away from the way I feel about you, JJ. Because I *do* feel for you. More than anyone else has ever made me feel."

The word-vomit spilling out of Rex's mouth made Jordan's heart thud its way up into his throat, and he buried his face in the taller man's neck again, another wave of tears springing in his eyes. "I feel the same way," he said, his voice muffled.

"Yeah?"

"Yeah, it's actually really annoying."

"You're just annoyed you fell for someone as cool and interesting and complex and sexy as me. It's okay, you can say it."

When their laughter quieted down and the attendees began talking and trading numbers for future Meet Cute Club alerts, Jordan wiped his face and asked, "How did you even afford all this? Flying Patricia out must have cost a fortune. You didn't have to do all this..."

"First, I did. Hell, right now I'm wondering if I should've done more. Because you deserve more than just this. You deserve a lifetime supply of... I don't know, all the Harlequin books you want. You deserve to be the inspiration for a romance novel of your own. Maybe Patricia will take some notes and put you in a book of hers as a character."

Jordan's eyes went wide. "Stop, don't get my hopes up. A shout out is one thing. Being a character in the book would kill me."

Rex chuckled softly. "I'm just saying, if I could make all that happen, I would. I was supposed to use all the money I made from the garage sale on a new bike because, apparently, my old one is 'wack,' but I decided this was a worthier cause."

Hearing that insult to his bike put a smile on Jordan's face. "You shouldn't have used it all on me, Rex. You earned that money."

"Nah, it was Nana's stuff that I sold. Something tells me that she'd want me to spend it on you."

Rex knew his grandmother. She'd believed in love more than anything else. If it had been between getting a new bike and him showing Jordan how much he cared about him, there was no doubt in his mind which option she'd choose. He refused to disappoint her, even if she was no longer with him.

"Thank you, Rex," Jordan said, reaching up to hold the back of the man's neck. "I'm sorry for being mean to you when we fought. I shouldn't have brought up your dad."

"Maybe not, but it was the kick in the ass I needed. That man doesn't get to define me. He doesn't get to deprive me of a happy home *and* the man I love."

Jordan's brows went up in surprise. "You love me?"

"You serious?" Rex asked, scoffing. "Do I love you… The nerve."

Jordan laughed and planted a quick kiss on his lips. "I think I might love you, too."

"You think?"

"I dunno, I think all these kissing books have given me way too high expectations," he teased. The first time he'd ever met Rex, the man had chastised him for being obsessed with romance books, yet here he was now, putting together the best Meet Cute Club meeting anyone had ever seen.

"I'm already tired of your smart ass," Rex grunted.

"No, you're not," Jordan said between kisses. "You love me *and* my smart ass, remember?"

"Yeah, well now I'm rethinking it," he chuckled. "I also wanted to tell you something."

Rex's tone got serious, and for a moment, fear crossed Jordan's face. They were in the perfect moment right now. It felt like they were the only ones in the room, lost in a private conversation that everyone was smart enough not to interrupt. Whatever Rex wanted to tell him didn't sound good, and he braced himself for impact.

"What's wrong?"

"Nothing's wrong, it's just... I've been talking to the lady helping me sell the house. She says she talked to the buyer, and they're really interested in purchasing the place. They want to get it as quickly as possible. It'll take a few weeks to finalize everything and process the payment, but after Nana's place sells, there's no reason to stay around. I know you said you forgive me, but I need you to tell me to stay, JJ. I need you to give me a reason."

Rex's face contorted, and his voice grew soft in a way that Jordan had never seen before. It was as if every façade he'd put up was coming down, revealing the truth that Rex Bailey wasn't the impenetrable, sarcastic douchebag that he pretended to be. He was human like everyone else, and he just wanted reassurance. He wanted to be told that he was needed.

Jordan brought Rex's hand to his lips and kissed a knuckle. Then he placed Rex's hand on his chest. "I want you to stay. Stay in Sweet Rose, Rex. Don't leave me again, okay?"

Rex's brows knit together, and he looked as if he were barely fighting back tears of his own. Jordan kissed his hand again, and that's when Rex nodded slowly.

"Okay. I'll stay."

Rex pulled him close for a deeper kiss, and for a split

second, he lost himself in it, absorbing every little thing about Jordan. The way his curly hair felt between his fingers, and how the small of his back arched perfectly when Rex's arm slid around it. This was the kind of kiss to wipe any doubts from the minds of the indecisive. The kind of resolution he'd been convinced just wasn't in the cards for him.

He'd needed the idea of never having this again to make him realize that Jordan wasn't just a temporary thrill but rather an immovable part of his story that he didn't want to end. He wasn't going to leave Sweet Rose. He was going to stay his ass right where he belonged.

When they'd finally parted and rejoined the rest of the group, Jordan took a moment to introduce Rex and Patricia. She seemed delighted to have a chance to meet with the man responsible for this trip in person, and Rex was more than happy to take Jordan's phone to snap a few pictures. The room filled with music, and before long, the attendees began doing tiny little shuffles, dancing as they chatted.

Lana appeared by Jordan's side and stole him from Rex. "I wanted to talk to you for a second," she said.

"What's up?"

"Well, my mom and I tried pottery," she said, giving him a look that immediately clicked for him.

"That bad?"

"Turns out I'm not talented with my hands. Maybe that's why I'm single... Anyway, Mom says she still wants to do something with me every week, so I pitched the club. She told me we should've just gone to the Meet Cute Club meetings in the first place."

"So...you're coming back?" As great as the club was, without Lana, it had always felt like they were missing something. Adding her mother into the mix would only make things that much better.

"I'm coming back, and I'm bringing my mom with me!"

Jordan could only smile like a kid in a candy store. All of the members he'd had before Rex were all back together again, and now there would be even more new faces and new perspectives on the genre. The idea of branching out, exploring different stories with his new friends, and spending hours talking about their favorite books was the cherry on top of the day.

He'd finally done it. All he'd wanted was to make a club as important as Sherleen's. He wanted to reach as many people as she had, and with Rex's help and the help of every other member of the club, he'd done it. They'd done it.

Jordan stood back and watched as the attendees and his friends mingled and ate snack food, all of them there because of the books he loved. To most people, it might've been silly to feel proud of it. After all, they were just books.

But for Jordan, it was more than that. It was about more than the books. It was about the community surrounding them, and the interpersonal relationships that were built all because of a mutual love of stories. The friendships he'd made, and the love he'd almost lost. These books brought people together, people he never wanted to be away from. If it meant tolerating some snarky cashier at a bookstore smarting off about his taste in reading material for him to have all this, then so be it. It was worth it in the end.

Besides, who *didn't* love an opposites-attract romance?

About the author

Jack Harbon is your typical, eccentric twenty-something writing stories much more interesting than his real life. If he's not writing, he's either reading domestic thrillers about women in peril, watching trashy reality TV shows, or playing The Sims.

CPSIA information can be obtained
at www.ICGtesting.com
Printed in the USA
FSHW011533230720
72413FS

9 798629 865032